Kristy and the
Mystery Train

**Other books by
Ann M. Martin**

Leo the Magnificat
Rachel Parker, Kindergarten Show-off
Eleven Kids, One Summer
Ma and Pa Dracula
Yours Turly, Shirley
Ten Kids, No Pets
Slam Book
Just a Summer Romance
Missing Since Monday
With You and Without You
Me and Katie (the Pest)
Stage Fright
Inside Out
Bummer Summer

Kristy and the
Mystery Train

Ann M. Martin

AN
APPLE
PAPERBACK

SCHOLASTIC INC.
New York Toronto London Auckland Sydney

Cover art by Hodges Soileau

ISBN 0-590-69178-3

12 11 10 9 8 7 6 5 4 3 2   7 8 9/9 0 1 2/0

Printed in the U.S.A.   40

First Scholastic printing, June 1997

*The author gratefully acknowledges
Nola Thacker
for her help in
preparing this manuscript.*

Kristy and the
Mystery Train

CHAPTER 1

"No," I said. "No way."

"It won't hurt," Linny Papadakis argued. "It's not like anyone's going to burn one down the middle at a hundred miles an hour."

"Excellent," said eight-year-old Nicky Pike.

His sister Claire, who is five, puckered her forehead into a ferocious frown. "I don't want to be *burned*!" she cried. She paused, thought for a moment, and added, "And I don't want to be hit, either."

"You're not going to be," I assured her quickly. Claire has been known to throw a *wicked* temper tantrum. "Neither is Linny. Or Nicky. Or anyone."

The subject was baseball — baseball and books. Linny, who's nine, had been reading baseball books. In one of the books, he'd read about a ballplayer who used to step in front of pitches. When the pitch hit him, he'd be awarded an automatic walk to first base.

1

Needless to say, this was not a strategy I wanted to practice in our league.

What league is that? Well, I guess you could say we are in a league of our own. I'm the coach of Kristy's Krushers, a softball team made up of kids ranging from two to nine years old, with an average age of 5.83. The skill level of our team is as broad as the age spread. We play for fun, but that doesn't mean that we don't take our fun seriously. At the moment, however, Linny was taking it just a little too seriously, in my opinion. And I could tell by the stubborn look in his eye that he wasn't going to give up easily.

Abby Stevenson, my neighbor, fellow Babysitters Club member (more about that in a little while), and the assistant coach of the team, said, "Good thinking, though, Linny. You really did your homework."

Her praise did not placate Linny. He stuck out his lower lip almost as far as Claire's and scowled.

It was a beautiful day in Stoneybrook, Connecticut. School was out, and summer had begun. What better way to start a summer, I had reasoned, than by doing a little of the old ballpark shuffle, bopping to some baseline boogie-woogie, taking myself out to a ballgame. So I had called a Krushers softball practice.

"Why don't we work on a little baserunning," I said. We could stand to improve our baserunning, and it was a good way to help the kids use up some excess energy. And maybe prevent a fight.

Jackie Rodowsky, all heart and a pretty good softball player (in spite of the fact that he has more than earned the affectionate nickname "the Walking Disaster"), said, "Yeah! Baserunning!"

Several other kids added enthusiastic agreement to my suggestion — but Linny remained stubbornly silent.

I decided that once he started baserunning, he'd come around. "Linny, you run first," I said, grabbing the bat. "Now, who wants to field the balls?"

Several other kids flung up their hands and called, "Me, me, me!"

In a few minutes, we had our fielders and our runners in place.

"BatterbatterbatterbatterSWING!" chanted Abby as I raised the bat, tossed the ball in the air, and fungoed the first ball to my stepsister, Karen, at shortstop.

Whoa. I guess I'd better go back to the beginning and give you a play-by-play.

I'm Kristy — Kristy Thomas. I'm thirteen years old and I'm in the eighth grade at Stoneybrook Middle School. In addition to being the coach of the Krushers, I'm also president and founder of the Baby-sitters Club (keep reading for more info on that), as well as the oldest daughter in a very large blended family. In fact, I almost have enough people in my family to field an entire baseball team.

Karen, at shortstop, is my stepfather's daughter. She's seven. Her younger brother (my stepbrother), Andrew, who is four, is also a Krusher, as is my younger brother, David Michael. He's seven, too. Family members who are not on the team include my mother; my stepfather, Watson Brewer; my maternal grandmother, Nannie; my two older brothers, Charlie and Sam; my younger sister, Emily Michelle (who is adopted); our dog, Shannon; our cranky cat, Boo-Boo; other assorted pets; and our resident ghost, Ben Brewer.

I popped a fly into right field. Nicky circled under it, lost it in the sun, and dropped it off the tip of his glove.

"Play it out!" I called.

But Nicky didn't appear to hear me. He froze, glove outstretched, knees half bent, his eyes focused on something behind me.

Thoughts of the ghostly Ben Brewer crossed my mind. Had he come to haunt our team?

"Nicky!" I called.

Nicky started to trot in toward home plate. As he reached the infield, he broke into a run down the first base line.

4

"Nicky? Nicky, is something — "

"Hey!" Nicky shouted at the top of his lungs. "Hey! *Hey, Derek!*"

When they heard that, the other kids turned and looked, too. Then they all broke rank, running from the field, speeding past me toward the Mercedes-Benz station wagon nudged up to the curb at the edge of the park.

But I didn't need to see the Benz to know the score.

"What's going on?" asked Abby as we jogged after our truant team.

"It's Derek Masters," I said.

Abby's quick. She looked at the Benz, she looked at the crowd of excited kids, and she looked at me. "Derek Masters? As in, Derek Masters the kid TV and movie star?"

"The very same," I said. "He filmed his TV movie *Little Vampires* right here in good old Stoneybrook."

Abby raised her eyebrows. "Rats. I thought when I moved to Stoneybrook that I was the most monster star this town had ever seen."

I groaned and rolled my eyes. "Derek's a star, but he's a cool kid," I said. By the time I reached the station wagon, the whole team had crowded around it, talking and laughing. I saw Derek's mother at the steering wheel. She waved at me, smiling.

"Let me out!" Derek said, laughing himself,

as he tried to push open the door of the car. At last, with Nicky's help, he managed to swing the door open and slide out.

He and Nicky grinned at each other. Nicky has been Derek's Stoneybrook best friend ever since Derek moved here.

"Are you here to make another movie?" Karen asked.

"How long can you stay?" asked Nicky.

"You want to practice with us?" asked Claire.

But before Derek could answer, the back door of the Benz, next to where I was standing, squeezed open. I stepped back, and another boy, who looked about Derek's age, climbed out.

"Are you a movie star, too?" I heard someone ask.

"Wait a minute," I said. "Everyone be quiet for just a minute and let Derek answer."

Derek flashed his big-screen grin. Even though he is just a kid, you can see that he has what people call star quality. "Thanks, Kristy," he said. "Nicky, everybody, this is Greg Raskin. He and I are in school together in California. Greg, this is Nicky, my Stoneybrook best friend. And Kristy, world-famous baby-sitter. And my other Stoneybrook friends."

Greg might not have been a star, but he had the same sort of advanced self-confidence that

Derek exhibited. He was just slightly taller than Derek, with straight brown hair cut long, almost chin length. He had brown eyes and was dressed in baggy shorts, a blindingly purple T-shirt, and surf shoes.

"Hi," he said. "I'm glad to meet you."

"Are *you* going to play ball with us?" asked Claire again.

Greg grinned at Claire. "I'd like to," he said, "but I think Derek and I have other plans right now."

Derek nodded. "I called your house, and your mother said you guys were all here," he said to Nicky. "So we stopped by to tell you the news."

"What news?" asked Karen, her blue eyes growing huge behind her glasses. "You're going to make another TV movie in Stoneybrook?"

Shaking his head, Derek said, "No, I'm afraid not. But I just finished a Hollywood movie. It's called *Night Train to Charleston*. It's about a murder on a train. I play a runaway who's hidden aboard the train. I see something that proves the woman who is framed for the murder isn't the murderer. Unfortunately, the murderer also sees me."

"Awesome," said Linny.

"I hope so," said Derek modestly. "It's a big part, and this is a major motion picture. Anyway, it premieres in Charleston, South Carolina, next week. And as part of the publicity for the movie, the entire cast and crew is going to ride on a special train, with sleeping cars and a dining car and everything set up to look like the one in the movie. It's going from Boston to Charleston. We're also going to reenact a few scenes on the train."

"Cool," said Linny.

"That's not the best part. The best part is that I can take a couple of friends along. So I wanted you to come, Nicky."

"All right!" Nicky shouted. "Yyyesss!"

"I know you'll have to ask your parents," Derek said. "I'll call you tonight with all the information."

"That's great, Derek," I said.

"I think so, too," he said.

Everyone started talking at once then, and Abby and I watched and listened as Derek fielded questions like a pro. After a few minutes Mrs. Masters leaned across the seat and said, "We're on kind of a tight schedule, Derek. We better go."

"We're glad you stopped by," I said to Derek. "Nice to meet you, Greg. 'Bye, Mrs. Masters."

"Talk to you tonight, Derek!" said Nicky.

Practicing softball after that wasn't easy, and not just because all the Krushers were distracted by Derek's visit. I have to admit, I couldn't stop thinking about his news, either. When practice ended, I was almost glad it was over.

As I gave everybody the postpractice pep talk and promised to schedule another practice soon, my eyes met Abby's. I knew she and I were thinking the same thing.

We had some very interesting news for the Wednesday meeting of the Baby-sitters Club later that afternoon.

CHAPTER 2

"This meeting of the Baby-sitters Club will now come to order, and do I have some news for you!" I said, all in one breath.

"*We*, Kristy. Do *we* have some news for you," Abby corrected her.

The clock read exactly 5:30, and the seven regular members of the BSC were gathered, as usual, in Claudia Kishi's room. Claudia is the vice-president of the BSC, one of the original members, and the only one of us who has her own telephone line.

That's why we meet in her room. Her phone line is our business number, which makes it easier for clients to reach us, and it also means that we don't annoy anyone by tying up a family phone with club business.

But I better begin at the beginning. The Baby-sitters Club (also known as the BSC) is a group of nine people (plus an honorary member) who all love to baby-sit: me; Claudia;

Mary Anne Spier, our secretary; Stacey McGill, our treasurer; Abby, our alternate officer; Jessica Ramsey and Mallory Pike, our junior officers; and Shannon Kilbourne and Logan Bruno, our associate members, who take any overflow business we have. Shannon and Logan weren't there that afternoon because associate members don't have to attend every meeting. And our honorary member, Dawn Schafer, wasn't there either, because she's moved to California, where she's in a West Coast version of the BSC called the We ♥ Kids Club. But the rest of us were present. It's one of the rules. Regular members have to attend meetings, which are held from five-thirty until six every Monday, Wednesday, and Friday afternoon. Clients know they can reach us then to set up baby-sitting jobs, so it's top priority for all of us to be present — unless one of us has something else important to do, such as baby-sit.

I thought up the Baby-sitters Club one night when I was listening to my mother phone sitter after sitter, trying to find someone to take care of David Michael. That's when it hit me: Wouldn't it be great if parents could make just one phone call and reach several sitters all at once?

I told my idea to my best friend, Mary Anne, and my other good friend, Claudia (we've all

11

known each other practically our whole lives).
Claudia told her new friend, Stacey, and we organized the BSC. It was clearly a brilliant idea
(I don't believe in false humility) because in no
time we had more work than we could handle.
Dawn soon joined us, followed by Logan, Mallory, Jessi, and Shannon.

When Dawn moved back to California, we
quickly realized we needed another full-time
baby-sitter on board. At about the same time,
Abby and her twin sister, Anna, moved in
down the street from me. We asked both of
them to join the BSC. Anna decided not to, but
Abby accepted and became our newest member.

Besides regular attendance at meetings, we
have a few other rules. We pay dues once a
week, on Mondays. The dues go toward Claudia's phone bill, our baby-sitting supplies, and
gas money for my brother Charlie, who drives
Abby and me to meetings. Members also have
to keep our BSC notebook up-to-date, and keep
up-to-date on what's in it. We write about each
and every baby-sitting job in the notebook, and
everybody reads it once a week. That way, we
stay on top of changes in the lives of our regular clients — who has learned to roller-skate, or
who has developed an allergy — and we can
pick up new ideas and coping strategies, too.

We also have a record book, in which we

keep track of our jobs and schedules. Mary Anne is in charge of that (she's never, ever made a mistake). Recently we began a mystery notebook, too. When we found ourselves involved in yet another mystery (while we were on what we thought would be an ordinary winter ski trip), we realized that we needed a central place to keep track of clues.

Each BSC member also has a Kid-Kit. Kid-Kits (invented by me) are basically cardboard boxes that we decorate and fill with things such as old puzzles, books, and toys. We use some of our dues to replenish the kits as needed, adding stickers or markers or paper. We don't take the kits to every job, but they are super icebreakers with new charges and perfect when a child is sick in bed or stuck inside due to bad weather.

That's about it. Pretty simple, isn't it? We don't need a lot of complicated rules because we are so good at what we do. In fact, we hardly ever have to try to drum up new clients. Our excellent reputation brings us all the business we can handle.

I think one of the reasons we work so well together is that we are all so different. Our differences cause problems sometimes, but they also mean that we have fun. And we are unbeatable at solving problems (and mysteries).

For example, Mary Anne and I are best

friends and we couldn't be more different. Physically we look similar. We are both short (actually, I'm the shortest person in our class) and have brown hair and brown eyes. And we both live in blended families.

But I've always lived in a large family. My father left us when David Michael was little. Back then, we lived in a small house on Bradford Court, next door to Mary Anne and across the street from Claudia. Charlie, Sam, David Michael, and I all had to pitch in and help out, and I learned to be responsible and to speak up for myself early on.

Not long ago, Mom met Watson Brewer. They fell in love and got married, and we moved away from Bradford Court . . . into a mansion. It's true. Watson is a real, live millionaire, and his house has plenty of room for everybody.

Mary Anne, on the other hand, lived alone with her father for many years, because her mother died when Mary Anne was a baby. Mary Anne's father was extremely strict and treated her like a child, even when she wasn't one anymore. He insisted that she wear pigtails and little-girl jumpers, for one thing. But she finally convinced him she had begun to grow up, and he agreed to give her room to make more of her own decisions, from how she wore her hair to more important things.

Which proves that although Mary Anne is very shy and very sensitive (unlike me), she is also stubborn (like me, as any of my friends will tell you). It wasn't easy to make her father see that she was growing up, but she did. Now she has a trendy new haircut, a kitten named Tigger, and even a boyfriend — Logan Bruno, our fellow baby-sitter.

She also has some new family members. Not long after Dawn Schafer moved here, she and Mary Anne discovered that Dawn's divorced mom and Mary Anne's widowed dad had been high school sweethearts. The girls reintroduced them, and before long, Dawn and Mary Anne became stepsisters! So Mary Anne and her dad left Bradford Court, too, to move in with Dawn and her mom.

Now Mary Anne lives in a possibly haunted house, with a real secret passage and a barn, near the edge of town. Dawn doesn't live there anymore, though. She realized that she missed California too much, so she went back to live with her father. We all miss Dawn, and we stay in touch as much as possible.

Mary Anne misses Dawn the most. After all, Dawn was not only Mary Anne's stepsister but her other best friend. I admit, I was jealous when they first became friends, but once I got to know Dawn, I couldn't help liking her.

Dawn is basically easygoing, though she has

a stubborn side, too. She is tall and has pale blue eyes and bleach-blonde hair. She likes surfing and sunshine, has two holes pierced in each ear, and is a vegetarian. She doesn't eat sugar or junk food very often, and she's made us all realize how important it is to recycle and not let people wreck the environment.

The BSC has another tall, thin, blonde, health-conscious member: Stacey. She's our treasurer because she's a math whiz. Her real name is Anastasia Elizabeth McGill (but you better not call her that!). She was born and raised in New York City.

Stacey's parents are divorced, and her father still lives in New York. Like Mary Anne, Stacey had to convince her parents to ease up on their overprotective routine. Their concern stemmed from a different cause: diabetes.

Diabetes is a condition in which your body doesn't make enough of a necessary substance called insulin. Practically speaking, it means that your blood sugar has to be carefully controlled. Stacey has to be extremely careful about what she eats, and she has to give herself insulin injections every day. If she doesn't, she could become very sick.

Maybe because she's from New York, and maybe because she has had to deal with diabetes, Stacey is a little more mature than the rest of us. She's also one of the most fashionable members of the BSC. Today, for example, while I was in my standard uniform of jeans, T-shirt, and sneakers, and Abby, Mary Anne, Jessi, and Mallory were all sporting casual looks involving shorts or jeans, Stacey was wearing an oversized butter-colored linen shirt that matched her hair, which was pulled back into a sleek French braid. Her baggy chino shorts were rolled up to exactly the same length on each leg, above the knee. Her sandals had cork soles, which made her look even taller and more elegant.

Claudia and Stacey are best friends, and Claudia is very trendy, too. But as with our other best-friend pairs, Stacey and Claud have plenty of differences. Claudia's look is less New York elegant and more funky-artistic.

That's because Claudia is an artist. Unlike Stacey, who is good at all subjects, not just math, Claudia thinks school is basic torture and she doesn't do well in it at all. What she *does* excel in is art. She's already won prizes for her work, and she plans to be a professional artist someday.

Claudia's artistic eye shows in the ways she combines colors and shapes in her clothes. Today she was in bright mode: red shorts, a purple crop top over a longer red-and-white-striped muscle shirt, purple socks, and red high-tops laced with red-and-white-striped shoelaces. Her hair was pulled up to one side with a knot of red and purple scrunchies, and her earrings were shiny red apples.

Not everyone could have looked good in that. But Claudia, with her long black hair, perfect creamy skin, and dark almond-shaped eyes (she's Japanese-American), looked terrific.

One more difference between Stacey and Claudia: Claudia is a junk-food gourmet. She keeps all kinds of bad goodies hidden strategically around her room, where her parents can't find them (they don't want her to eat junk food, and they don't want her to read Nancy Drew books for some reason, so she hides those, too). Claudia always shares her hidden treats with us at BSC meetings, along with pretzels and popcorn and other healthier snacks for Stacey.

Two other best friends in the BSC are Mallory and Jessi. As junior officers, they concentrate on daytime sitting jobs. That's because they are both eleven and in sixth grade, so they aren't allowed to sit at night yet, except for their own brothers and sisters.

Mallory has had *plenty* of baby-sitting experience. The oldest of eight children, she has four brothers (including Nicky), three of whom are identical triplets, and three sisters (including Claire).

Like all of her sisters and brothers, Mallory

has pale skin, blue eyes, and hair in the chestnut brown range, although in Mal's case it is more of a reddish brown. To her eternal despair she wears glasses and braces. She wants to lose the braces (but her parents and her dentist won't let her) and is saving her money for contact lenses. She likes to write and draw and wants to be a children's book author and illustrator someday. And she loves horses and horse stories, interests she shares with Jessi.

Jessi and Mal have other things in common, too: Like Mal, Jessi is the oldest kid in her family. And both girls have pet hamsters.

But Jessi is from a smaller family. She has one younger sister, Becca, and one baby brother, John Philip, Jr. (nicknamed Squirt), plus her mother, father, and her aunt Cecelia (who helps take care of the family). And Jessi's ambition is to be a professional ballerina. She takes special dance classes after school in Stamford, gets up every morning at 5:29 exactly to practice on the *barre* set up in her basement, and has already danced important roles in several ballets. Although Jessi was dressed as casually as all of us except Claudia and Stacey, her clothes definitely gave away clues about her interest in ballet. She was wearing an old, faded pink leotard that made her brown skin and brown eyes glow, and her black hair was pulled back into a dancer's bun. She carries herself like a dancer, too — very gracefully and with perfect posture.

Our newest member, Abby, is not yet close to anyone in particular, although, of course, we are all friends. She and her mother and twin sister, Anna, moved here after Mrs. Stevenson earned a big promotion at her job in New York City. Abby's father was killed in a car wreck a few years ago. She hardly ever talks about him.

But don't make the mistake of thinking Abby is quiet or shy. The opposite is true. She is very opinionated. I noticed this right away, when she started challenging everything I said. Okay, maybe she didn't challenge *everything*, but the point is, Abby is not shy about sharing her thoughts.

I don't always agree with her, and she and I don't always get along. But I respect Abby, and I like her. And we do have some things in common. For example, we are both sports fans, big time. I can watch any game, anytime, anywhere. And I like to play softball so much that I tried out for, and made, the SMS girls' softball team.

If it's possible, Abby is even more athletic than I am, hard as that is to admit. She is a little taller than I am, with brown hair and brown eyes. Sometimes she wears glasses and sometimes she wears contacts, depending on her mood. She's a soccer fanatic who can tell you the names of every single player on the U.S. women's soccer team. Plus, she's a player. She was captain of her team back on Long Island, and she joins every pickup game she sees.

Abby never walks when she can jog. Even when it's not soccer season, she's in training, "just in case." She's recently added a new item to the list of sports she admires (although she hasn't taken it up yet): swimming. That's because some Olympic swimmers have asthma and allergies, just as Abby does.

Abby is allergic to all kinds of things, from milk to cat litter. And she always carries two inhalers with her (one over-the-counter, one prescription), in case she has an asthma attack. But as you might guess, she doesn't let her asthma or her allergies slow her down.

And nothing could slow down Abby's sense of humor. She loves jokes and makes the most awful puns in the world, sometimes so quickly that she's begun a new joke before I've figured out the last one.

Another BSC jock is Logan, which is one of the reasons he's an associate member instead of a full-time one. He's a good enough student, but basically, as far as he's concerned, school means sports: baseball, football, volleyball, track, you name it. With all those practices and games, he doesn't have a whole lot of extra time for baby-sitting. Some people have been deceived by Logan's soft Southern accent and good manners — and his membership in the BSC — into thinking they can push him around. Wrong. Logan stands up for what he believes in.

Shannon is the only member of the BSC who doesn't go to SMS. She's a student at a private school in Stoneybrook, and although she's as busy as Logan, her involvement in school activities is more academic. She's in tons of clubs, including the French club, she's the only eighth-grader in the astronomy club, and she earns practically straight A's. When I first moved to this neighborhood and met Shannon (she lives across the street), I thought she was a big snob (she didn't think much of me, either). But after we got to know each other, we became friends. In fact, Shannon's dog, Astrid, who is a Bernese mountain dog, is the mother of our puppy, Shannon. David Michael named Shannon the puppy after Shannon our neighbor and associate BSC member.

So there you have the BSC. If you'd walked into Claudia's room just then, you'd have seen Claudia tearing into a bag of chips, Mary Anne with the club record book open on her lap, and Jessi and Mallory sitting on the floor, staring at Abby and me. Stacey was smoothing some stray hairs into her French braid, while glancing from me to Abby with one eyebrow raised.

I was in the director's chair, where I always sit during BSC meetings, and Abby was propped against the dresser, her arms folded, watching everyone else watch us.

"News? What news?" demanded Claudia.

"You'll never guess who showed up at Krushers practice today," I said.

"Kristy!" wailed Mary Anne. "That's not fair."

"We'll give you a clue," Abby said. "He may not be an all-star, but you could definitely call him a star."

"Babe Ruth?" Claudia guessed.

"Babe Ruth is dead!" I exclaimed.

"I know. So he can't be an all-star, but you could still call him a star, right?" said Claudia.

"She's right," Mallory pointed out.

"Okay, I'll tell you. It's — "

Just then the phone rang. I scooped it up, unable to resist the temptation to prolong the suspense a little more. "Baby-sitters Club."

"May I please speak to Kristy Thomas?" said a voice I'd heard before. I couldn't quite place it, but the next words solved *that* mystery. "This is Mr. Masters, Derek's father."

"Oh! Hi! This is Kristy," I said, sounding a lot calmer than I suddenly felt.

"Kristy. How are you? I'm glad I reached you." Mr. Masters went on to explain why he had called.

I listened closely, said "okay" a couple of

times, and then hung up the phone in a daze.

"*What?*" Claudia practically screamed.

"Check the book," I told Mary Anne. "See if we have three people who can take a job with nine kids for a three-day train ride from Boston, Massachusetts, to Charleston, South Carolina, beginning this Friday."

"Derek Masters," Abby guessed, looking smug.

"WHAT?!" Claudia did scream that time. So did everyone else. It took awhile for things to settle down enough for me to explain.

I generously let Abby tell how Derek had shown up at practice and invited Nicky to join him on the "Mystery Train" ride to promote his new movie.

Then I said, "But what Derek doesn't know is that Mr. Masters has decided that Derek can have not only Nicky and Greg, but four other friends on the train. As a surprise, Mr. Masters is going to invite four more of Derek's friends to go on the train ride. Plus Derek's brother Todd, and Todd's best friend will be along. Mr. Masters, who is also an executive producer for the film, is going to be too busy to keep an eye on all nine kids, and Mrs. Masters can't go at all, so Mr. Masters needs three sitters."

Trying to act calm and professional, Mary Anne flipped the pages of the record book. She sighed and looked up. "Jessi, Claud, Mal, and

I have a previous engagement," she said.

Claudia groaned. "I know. Helping with the opening of the summer season at Greenbrook." The Greenbrook Club used to be a ritzy, exclusive country club. It recently reopened, with far more welcoming policies toward the general public.

Mal shrugged philosophically. "I have a feeling my parents wouldn't have let me be a baby-sitter on a long-distance train ride."

"Same here," Jessi said.

Still in her professional mode, Mary Anne poised her pencil above the page. "That leaves Kristy, Stacey, and Abby, and possibly Shannon. Logan is at baseball camp this week."

"Well, if Mom and Watson say yes, count me in," I said.

"Ditto my parents," said Stacey.

"I can do it," said Abby. No one asked her if she had to check with her mom. Abby has a lot more freedom and independence than the rest of us. She'd ask her mom, of course, but it would be almost more of a formality than a request for permission to go.

"Good," said Mary Anne. She wrote our names down, along with the information Mr. Masters had given me.

At the same time, Mallory reached into her backpack. "The Mystery Train," she said, pulling out another notebook. "Do you think I need to start a section in the mystery notebook for it?"

"Oh, come on, Mal. They're only calling it the Mystery Train because the movie is a mystery," I said.

"Seriously," said Claudia. "Just because Derek led us into one mystery, doesn't mean he's going to get us into another. Right?"

"What is this Derek-mystery connection? You guys have talked about this before, but no one's ever explained," Abby said.

"It's all written up here," said Mallory. "The mystery of Kristy and the vampires." She patted the notebook and handed it over to Abby.

"Read all about it," Jessi joked. "Read how the vampires came to our little town. And more."

"But seriously, folks," I said, as the phone rang again. "I don't think we have to worry about any kind of mystery. Anyway, the train ride will be exciting enough without one."

It turned out that I was right about the train ride's being exciting.

But was I ever wrong about not having a mystery on board!

CHAPTER 3

"Mallory would have liked to see Louisa May Alcott's house," Stacey said, studying the Boston guidebook. "Alcott wrote *Little Women*, you know."

"There's an aquarium," suggested Nicky.

Mom said, "Don't forget the Children's Museum."

"No!" said Linny Papadakis and Buddy Barrett. Buddy added, "It's too much like school."

I met my mother's eyes across the fancy table and we both smiled. I like going to museums now and seeing historic sites. I've liked it ever since we took a class trip to Salem, Massachusetts, where we studied the witch hunts that took place in Colonial America — and found ourselves involved in a creepy mystery.

See what a little interest in history can lead to?

But I didn't say that aloud. Nicky and Derek's other Stoneybrook friends, Buddy Barrett, James Hobart, Linny, and David Michael, were already excited enough without the mention of crimes and mysteries. As a matter of fact, I thought that David Michael's uncharacteristic silence just now was due to excitement.

David Michael is friends with Derek, but he isn't Derek's best friend. I suspected that Mr. Masters had included David Michael in the invitation as much for my sake as for my brother's. On the other hand, since Derek spends much of his time in California, on the set of his television series, he doesn't have *that* many close friends in Stoneybrook. So it worked out well.

We'd arrived in Boston on Friday evening. "We" was Stacey, Abby, me, Mom, Watson, Nicky, Linny, Buddy, James, and David Michael. Mr. Masters had put us all up at a swank hotel overlooking Boston Harbor. Although we had arrived late, we were too excited to settle in right away, so Mom and Watson had gone with us to explore the Faneuil Hall/Quincy Market area nearby. Looking up at Faneuil Hall Marketplace while people swarmed around us, it was hard to imagine this two-story, bronze-domed building as the "Cradle of Liberty" described in the guidebooks. But it had been exactly that. Mass meetings of patriots had convened there during the pre-revolutionary period. Now it, along with two other restored buildings, housed what seemed like hundreds of shops and restaurants.

Stacey plunged into one shop after another while we trailed along, taking in the sights, followed by the boys, who were practically spinning in circles trying to see everything at once. But then the door of a restaurant opened, swamping us with delicious aromas, and we realized how hungry we were. We chose a seafood restaurant and pigged out on chowder and seafood. After that, it was easy for Mom and Watson to persuade the boys — and us — that it was time to go back to the hotel and get some sleep.

I woke up early the next morning to . . . Abby breath. She was standing next to my bed, in the bedroom we baby-sitters were sharing. (The five boys had the room next to us, connected to our room by a door, which we'd left open. Beyond their door, another door opened into Mom's and Watson's room.) But Abby wasn't just standing. She was also leaning over and staring at me.

"Wh-at?" I muttered groggily. I wasn't used to staying up so late, or to eating quite so many clams for dinner, I had to admit.

"This hotel happens to have an *excellent* exercise room *with* a sauna *and* a masseuse," Abby informed me in an urgent whisper, in order not to wake Stacey. "You do want to check them out, don't you?"

As my eyes began to focus, I realized that Abby was already dressed in her sweats and sneaks. I also recognized the rays coming in the window as very early sunlight.

But I wasn't about to admit to Abby that I wanted to sleep. She'd never let me hear the end of it. "Give me a minute," I muttered and staggered out of bed.

It *was* an excellent exercise room. Abby did sets of weights while I put in some miles, alternating between the NordicTrack and the treadmill. We even hung around in the sauna, which we had all to ourselves — not surprisingly, considering it was practically dawn. However, the masseuse was not yet on duty, much to my secret relief.

Now everybody was up and dressed and sitting at the breakfast table with Mom and Watson. We were trying to decide what to do with the time we had free before going to the train station. The early morning workout hadn't tired me out after all, I realized. I was full of energy and very hungry.

Looking at the Fearsome Five (as I had secretly dubbed them), I could see that they, too, had recovered from the exhaustion of the previous evening. With a long train ride ahead, what they needed was a little workout of their own.

"What about a walking tour?" I suggested. "I saw a sign in the lobby for one that meets in about twenty minutes. It'll be over by eleven, and we'll have plenty of time to meet the train at one."

"I'd like that," said James. "We've even heard about Boston in Australia."

"It's a nice little town," said Stacey.

I'd call Boston a pretty big town myself, but for Stacey, even Boston is small, compared to her hometown.

We walked the walk — all the way through Boston, it seemed to me, although according to our maps, we only went through Boston Common (which the guide called "The Common"), the Public Garden, and Beacon Hill. We learned that The Common is forty-eight acres and was set aside in 1634 as a cow pasture and training field, and is available still for the same purposes by law. We didn't see any cows, though.

In the Public Garden we all oohed and ahhed over the formal gardens, but the swan boats in the pond were the biggest hit with the Fearsome Five. We didn't ride in them, though. Our guide, a dark-haired pre-med student at Boston University, had other plans for us.

31

She kept us going at a good pace, telling us something about almost every building we passed. The next big crowd pleaser was the John Hancock Observatory, on the sixtieth floor of John Hancock Tower. From it we could see what seemed like all of Boston and most of Massachusetts. We also took in a multimedia show about Boston's history.

By then, even Abby and I were slowing down. After touring the John F. Kennedy National Historic Site, our group left the tour and strolled back to the hotel for a little snack (and a little rest).

Seeing Derek at the train station immediately revived everyone, especially when we caught his reaction to the sight of us. He was standing inside a roped-off area in the train station, with what I think of as his "politely interested" expression. But when he saw us, genuine excitement lit up his face. He said something to the short, intense-looking woman with creamy brown skin and short black hair standing next to him, and then headed for the rope, the woman following, stopping every few steps to talk in a cellular phone. "It's okay," Derek said to a guard, who had just demanded to see our identification, "they're with me."

Magic words. Suddenly the guard was smiling, unhooking the rope, and almost bowing as he led us to the collection of famous and powerful people waiting to ride the Mystery Train and celebrate the opening of *Night Train to Charleston*.

"Buddy! David Michael! Linny! James! What are you guys doing here? This is great!" cried Derek.

Mr. Masters hadn't detached himself from the group he'd been talking to. Instead he'd brought it with him. "Perfect timing," he declared. "Well, Derek, this should make the trip more interesting. Are you surprised?"

"Yes! This is *excellent*," exclaimed Derek. A light flashed, and we all turned to see a photographer squatting nearby. Next to him was a tall, thin, blonde woman with pale skin, wearing a creamy pink silk suit. She was a dead ringer for Stacey, except, of course, she looked older. A tag attached to the lapel of the suit identified her as PRESS.

Derek hadn't even appeared to notice the flash of the camera. Neither had Mr. Masters or any of the people with him. But the short woman with the cellular phone had. She turned, flipped the phone shut, smiled, and hurried toward the photographer and the reporter. "Jane," I heard her say. "Jane Atlantic!"

"Let's get everybody introduced here," said Mr. Masters.

Derek picked up on this cue like the pro he is and handled the introductions as calmly as any adult.

We met a tall, much-too-thin man with an explosion of rusty hair around a bald spot on the top of his head. The bald spot was covered with freckles. He was Rock Harding, the director.

"They in the business?" he asked Mr. Masters as Derek said our names.

"No, Rock," said Mr. Masters patiently. "I told you. They're friends of Derek's."

"Oh," said Mr. Harding. "Nice meeting you, kids," he added, looking vaguely into the air over our heads. "Ah, if you'll excuse me."

"Remind me to tell you what I read about *him*," Stacey whispered in my ear.

A round, nondescript man with square glasses, a ruddy complexion, and a receding hairline turned out to be Ronald Pierce, who wrote the screenplay for the movie. He surveyed us through his glasses, said, "Ah, yes, delighted, delighted," and then appeared to withdraw into a world of his own.

The small, intense woman who herded the photographer and the Stacey look-alike over to us turned out to be the publicist for the movie. Her name was Anne Arbour, and I couldn't help but compare her to the hyperactive, high-heel-clad, overdressed publicist from Derek's movie *Little Vampires*. I decided that Ms. Arbour, who was in khakis, a cropped jacket, and a striped T-shirt, was a big improvement. For one thing, she got my name right the first time she said it, and she sounded as if she meant it when she said she was glad we could be there.

Nevertheless, her eyes kept moving, as if she were always on the alert for the perfect photo opportunity. But then, I've noticed that a *lot* of people who work in movies do that. It's as if they don't exist unless they're in front of a camera — any camera. Meanwhile, the photographer snapped photos, and the reporter, Jane Atlantic, talked into a micro-recorder.

Missing from our welcoming party but conspicuous in the crowd were the two stars of the movie, Benjamin Athens and Elle San Carlos. I didn't need Stacey whispering in my ear to know that Athens, who has blue eyes and black hair that demanded even *my* attention, has been dubbed "The Sexiest Man on the Planet" by *People* magazine, or that he has a reputation for being difficult and out of control. When gossip columns write about the "major new star who apparently travels from hotel room to hotel room with his own personal wrecking crew," everyone knows it's Athens.

I just hoped he didn't decide to wreck the train. At the moment, he seemed to be all charm as the cameras flashed and flashed.

Next to him, Elle San Carlos more than held her own. Not only was she as tall as Benjamin, but her silver gray eyes and sleek cap of red hair were a knockout combination. She moved with an easy self-confidence and grace that Benjamin didn't have.

"She got her start as a stuntwoman," Abby muttered.

I looked at Abby in surprise. Keeping up with the rich and famous is not characteristic of her. Her next words explained it. "Elle was excellent at hoops. An NCAA all-star at Old Dominion in Virginia."

Trust Abby to have the sports stats on a movie star.

As we watched, Elle's head turned and the smile on her face suddenly became fake-looking. At the same moment, Ms. Arbour detached herself from our group and headed for the two stars. In another moment, she was herding them, and their attendant photographers toward the steps of the train.

Jane Atlantic was hard on their heels. "Ms. San Carlos!" she called out. "What about your husband? Do you have a comment about the divorce? Would you and Benjamin call this 'the honeymoon train'?"

Elle kept walking, her shoulders stiff, her head high. Ms. Arbour turned and said, "We agreed before giving you a press pass on the train, Jane — "

Jane snapped, "I'm a reporter. And a press pass on a train doesn't mean I'm not going to ask hard questions. I'm not here to write fluff. I want a story with some real bite to it!"

"Elle!" a voice cried.

Elle froze, then turned reluctantly. Why, I wondered, had she stopped for that one voice when so many people were calling her name? Ms. Arbour laid her hand on Elle's arm and spoke.

Elle shook her head and stepped away.

"Uh-oh," said Derek.

"What?" I asked as Elle stopped in front of an incredibly muscular blond man with brown eyes and an almost military haircut. He was slightly shorter than Elle.

"Elle's husband," Derek explained. "Charlie."

"Uh-oh," Abby echoed Derek.

We drifted closer, very casually.

Jane gestured frantically at her photographer, who was still taking pictures of our group. He turned and ran toward her.

Charlie reached out and clasped both of Elle's wrists. "Please," he said. "Please, Elle. I *love* you. He doesn't. He's just using you for publicity."

"At the moment," Elle said, "you're the one who's getting all the publicity."

"I don't care! I only care about you! About us!"

"We're through, Charlie." She pulled her wrists free.

"It's all his fault," Charlie cried. "Elle. Wait. Don't you see . . . you need me. Tell the truth, Elle. Tell the truth!"

"The truth? We were through *before* Benjamin," Elle answered. She turned on her heel and walked away as the cameras flashed and the tape recorders whirred.

"Elle! Elle, wait!" Charlie lunged after her. But two enormous guys in suits that were straining at the seams appeared out of nowhere. Each took one of Charlie's arms. He struggled against them for a moment, calling after Elle. Charlie was strong, but he was no match for them, and after a moment he stopped fighting.

An ugly look crossed his face. "You'll be sorry," he said, and I felt a chill down my spine.

But who was he looking at — Benjamin, or Elle, who had rejoined Benjamin? I couldn't tell, but I sure was glad he wasn't looking at me.

The guards led Charlie away, and we said good-bye to Mom and Watson then.

The train itself, an exact replica of the train from *Night Train to Charleston*, was deluxe. In the compartment Abby, Stacey, and I were sharing were fresh flowers in a little silver vase attached to red-and-silver-wallpapered walls. Heavy red curtains swathed the windows. We even had our own bathroom with a tiny shower!

"Cool, huh?" asked a voice from the doorway. It was Derek. "We're next door."

"All of you?" I gasped.

"Nah," Derek said. "Nicky, Greg, James, and I are in the compartment on one side of you, and David Michael, Linny, and Buddy are in the compartment on the other side of you. Todd's best friend, Daniel Pierce, and Daniel's father, Ronald — he's the screenwriter, remember? — are in the compartment just past Linny and Buddy. Todd and my dad are on the other side of my compartment."

"Good," said Abby, her tone faintly relieved.

I knew why. Nine kids in the same compartment offered an almost unlimited potential for mischief.

"Let's go check out the rest of the train," Derek said. "And find something to eat. It's *way* past lunchtime and I'm starved."

We found the dining car with no trouble. At the entrance to it, an attendant was handing out the programs for the mystery scenes that would be acted out on board. I took mine without looking at it. I was too busy taking in the surroundings, from the heavy tables and chairs in dark wood that matched the paneling, to the snowy white tablecloths and the silver and china that gleamed everywhere.

"Those aren't real gas fixtures," Derek said, pointing to the globes of frosted glass that lit the car. "They're electric."

"I'm relieved," I said.

The maître d' asked our names, checked her list, and then escorted us to a long table set up at the end of the dining car. "Welcome to the Mystery Train," she told us. "Your waiter will be with you shortly."

David Michael gave her a frightened look. "What if you just want a snack?" he said, his voice almost squeaking.

"You can order whatever you like," said the maître d', smiling at him reassuringly. "And of course we have a snack bar, referred to on the Mystery Train as the club car. There's a layout of the train in your program."

David Michael sank back in his chair, looking relieved.

I raised my program, opened it . . . and a small white piece of paper fell out with a single line photocopied onto it.

THE TRUTH WILL COME OUT — THERE'S NOTHING YOU CAN DO TO STOP ME.

Across from me, James said, "Here, what's this?" as a small strip of white paper slid out of his program.

Everyone had received the same message.

"I guess it's a fake clue," said Derek, sounding faintly puzzled. "You know, arranged by publicity to help put everybody in the mood. Anne's the one in charge of this trip."

The waiter arrived and handed around menus.

I took mine, but I didn't open it. I sat there, menu in one hand, scrap of paper clenched in the other.

A piece of paper that wasn't supposed to be in the program.

How did I know that? Because I was staring at Anne Arbour. And Anne Arbour was staring down at an identical piece of white paper. Her eyes had narrowed and her lips thinned to a furious line. She rose abruptly, crumpled the piece of paper in her fist, then strode angrily out of the dining car.

I knew then that we hadn't been given a phony clue. We'd been given a real threat.

But what did it mean? And even more important, I thought . . .

Who was it meant for?

CHAPTER 4

Saturday,

We didn't think we would have
to break out the mystery notebook
on this trip, but we were wrong.
Mal, forgive us, but we're having
to make do with paper we
borrowed from Mr. Masters. You
can edit our notes and add them
to the mystery notebook when we
return. If we return.

Ha. Ha. Just kidding. We hope....

"Everyone, save your clues," I said.

Fortunately, none of the kids asked any questions. And although Stacey and Abby gave me looks that said they would have a few questions later, they held their peace for the moment.

I stuffed my clue in my pocket and everyone else followed suit. Then our waiter glided over to us. As we gave him our orders, the train rolled smoothly out of the station, a lot more smoothly than Anne had when she stalked out of the dining car. I didn't say anything because I didn't want any of the kids (particularly Derek) to worry, but I had a distinctly uneasy feeling.

"This is *not* the New York City subway," Stacey joked. "I can tell because nobody fell down or made any unintelligible announcements."

"I can tell because this doesn't look like any train I've ever been on. If Mom could commute to work on a train like this, she'd love it," said Abby.

"Commute? I'd like to live on this train," Stacey answered.

"May we have anything we want to eat?" Daniel Pierce asked. Daniel turned out to be a smaller, stockier version of his father, except that his curly brown hair wasn't receding and he didn't need glasses.

I did a quick mental review of the instructions Mr. Masters had given us. Basically he had said, "You're in charge. We're here if you need help."

"Yes," I said to Daniel.

Stacey added quickly, "But *not* just dessert."

Daniel grinned. "Okay," he said. Although the menu was enormous, the food of choice turned out to be pizza (although the pizza toppings were what I considered to be Hollywood-style, such as goat cheese and marinated shrimp). We opted for one kid-style, with extra cheese; one with pepperoni and sausage; and one vegetarian, at Greg's request.

"You're a vegetarian?" asked Nicky, staring hard at Greg.

"Yeah," said Greg.

"Like Dawn," said Nicky.

Derek explained to Greg, "She's one of the Baby-sitters Club people, only she lives in California now."

"Is everybody in California a vegetarian?" asked Nicky.

"Not really," said Greg, unruffled.

For a moment, I wondered if Greg and Nicky weren't going to get along. After all, it isn't easy for a person's two best friends to meet for the first time (and I could remember all too well how much I had disliked Mary Anne's having both me and Dawn as best friends, at first). I resolved to keep an eye on the situation, just in case.

The doors to the dining car kept opening and closing, and delicious aromas kept pouring out. Various waiters soon followed, dressed alike in black pants, white T-shirts, and black cutaway vests. The vests were embroidered with the words NIGHT TRAIN TO CHARLESTON across the back and the word STAFF, in smaller letters, above a movie logo on the right front panel.

The waiters brought out all kinds of trays and bottles and dishes, including silver trays covered with high silver domes. Although the train swayed from side to side, sometimes tipping sharply as we rounded a curve, the waiters moved as surefootedly as cats. Their look-alike costumes gave the process the air of a choreographed dance.

"Very classy," commented Abby as she watched one of the silver-domed trays go by on its way to the other end of the dining car. "But somehow, I don't think that's our pizza."

"What do you bet it comes in a silver pizza pan, though," said Stacey.

The dining car was full by now. At the far

end, Benjamin Athens sat at a table with Mr. Masters, Jane Atlantic, and another member of the press.

Nearby, Elle was smiling and laughing, talking to Rock Harding and some other people I didn't know. Anne had returned to fill the empty seat she had so abruptly vacated, and I thought her watchfulness held a new element: fear.

I also noticed that Benjamin kept glancing in Elle's direction, as if he wished she were at the table with him. Elle, however, didn't seem to notice.

It was funny to be sitting at an elegantly set table, waiting to be served lunch, while houses and roads and shopping strips streamed by the windows outside. Even more unreal was the cast of characters. Who would have ever thought, when I came up with the idea for the Baby-sitters Club, that I would one day have a baby-sitting job on a train full of movie stars, headed for Charleston, South Carolina?

The waiter refilled our water glasses, never spilling a drop, and handed around our sodas.

"These glasses are *heavy*," said Buddy.

"They're weighted at the bottom," explained the waiter. "Most of the china and glassware is specially weighted to help prevent it from tipping or sliding when the train moves."

"Cool," said Linny.

"Cool," echoed David Michael.

The boys immediately began to check out the rest of the things on the table. The sugar bowls (which were filled with little cubes of sugar wrapped in paper that read NIGHT TRAIN TO CHARLESTON) were weighted, too, and so were the salt and pepper shakers.

"Check it out," Buddy cried. "The table even has a raised edge on it." Sure enough, under the tablecloth, we could feel a thin raised edge.

"I guess that helps keep the plates from sliding off," said Derek.

"Check *this* out," said Greg. "I think that's our pizza."

We all turned to watch the three enormous pizza trays (silver toned, but not silver) being carried toward our table.

The waiter put them down with a flourish.

We leaned forward expectantly.

Over at her table, Elle jumped up from her chair so quickly that, even as heavy as it was, it went crashing backward. She began to scream.

She wasn't the only one. Anne leaped up, too, holding her napkin to her lips, her face ashen.

When I saw what was wrong, I wanted to scream along with them.

The waiter had raised the lid of his silver-domed dish to reveal, nestled in a bed of carrots and potatoes . . .

A human hand.

Several things happened almost simultaneously. Benjamin swooped across the car and put his arms around Elle. She sagged against him, then straightened up, raising her chin as if to say, "The show must go on."

Jane ran to the table, raised her tape recorder to her lips, and began dictating, her fascinated, horrified gaze moving from Elle to the ghastly plate and back again.

Somehow I found myself halfway across the dining car — close enough to the grisly entrée to realize that it was made of rubber, and completely fake. I was also close enough to see the scrap of white paper Elle cautiously plucked from between the rubber fingers of the hand. She read it aloud in a resolute voice: " 'The truth will come out. There's nothing you can do to stop me.' "

Benjamin took the paper from her hand. "What? What does this mean? Is this your idea of publicity?" He waved the paper under Anne's nose.

I felt Stacey's hand on my arm, dragging me back. Turning, I saw the shocked faces of the kids, swallowed hard, and said, "Don't worry. It's not real. It's a fake hand, like they sell around Halloween."

"F/X," said Derek. "Sure. We should have guessed it was just some crummy fake." He managed to make it sound as if finding a fake hand on your dinner plate happened all the time, at least in Hollywood. What a pro he was!

"Eff ex?" asked Abby. "What does 'eff ex' mean, Derek? Everybody, sit down. Sit down, okay?"

Reluctantly our nine charges returned to their seats.

"Special effects. You write it eff, slash, ex. That's the movie term for it," said Derek. He smiled wanly. "Like when people go through glass windows, only it's not real glass. It's really thin and it's safe but you add in the sound of real glass breaking. I guess this is one publicity stunt that didn't work out."

David Michael said faintly, "Publicity stunt."

From the look on Anne's face, I didn't think it was a publicity stunt. She had taken the paper from Benjamin's hand and they were arguing fiercely, but in low tones.

Mr. Masters had managed to maneuver Jane Atlantic off to one side. Rock Harding, the director, was sprawled out dramatically in his chair. In one corner, I saw Daniel's father leaning forward, avidly taking in the whole scene, probably making notes for his next screenplay. The waiter had reappeared with the chef in tow, and they were talking, with excited gestures, to Elle.

No, it wasn't a publicity stunt. I didn't need

to hear the discussions going on around me to realize that. But I didn't say so.

"Outrageous," I heard one voice say, and then Benjamin's voice rang out. "Someone will pay for this!" He and Elle were walking out of the dining room. Anne was right behind them.

Jane Atlantic broke free and followed. "So this *wasn't* planned?" she asked triumphantly. She thrust out her tape recorder. "Elle, tell me, who would do this to you? Do you think your husband is behind it? After all, you and Charlie met when you were both stuntpeople."

Anne quickly intervened. "I think you will agree that as stunts go, this was pretty amateur. Someone's idea of a joke."

She turned to address the dining car, blocking Jane at the same time so that Benjamin and Elle could make their escape. The living quarters were off limits to the press.

Raising her voice, Anne said, "Everybody, please go back to enjoying your lunch. We have a lot of things planned to make this a fun trip. I hope you'll forget about this tasteless practical joke."

"I bet that hand *was* pretty tasteless," Abby said.

We all looked at her. Then, maybe from the tension, we cracked up. When the laughing had subsided, it seemed that everyone's appetite had mysteriously returned. We set to work on our pizzas, and soon almost everybody else in the dining car had gone back to eating. I noticed, however, that all of the entrées brought out after that arrived uncovered.

I ate with an air of calm I didn't feel, trying to set a good example. After all, that was part of my job as a baby-sitter.

My brain, however, was churning. We definitely had a mystery on our hands.

Despite all the excitement, Derek maintained his cool. But he had barely swallowed his last bite of pizza when Anne bore down upon us.

She nodded at everyone but spoke to Derek. "Could you go around and make nice to the press?" she said. "Elle and Benjamin are — unavailable — so as third lead in the movie . . ."

"Of course," said Derek. He folded his napkin and rose to follow Anne.

A moment later he had slipped into the chair next to Jane and two other reporters. From there we watched him move on to a tall woman with wraparound dark glasses and a man dressed entirely in black, including his high-tops.

Suddenly, Derek ducked beneath a table, pulling the tablecloth over him.

"What's he doing?" asked Nicky, sounding alarmed.

Greg grinned at Nicky. "It's a scene from the movie. He's hiding from the murderer. The murderer isn't sure who saw him, just that it's a kid, so he's trying to check out all the kids on the train."

"I guess not *all* of the scenes are going to be acted out in the stage car," said Stacey, referring to a car that had been set up with special lighting and seating and a stage at one end.

The waiter had reappeared with a dessert menu. Although we had done serious damage to the pizza, all of the boys managed to find room for the dessert special, Mystery Cupcakes, which turned out to be chocolate cupcakes with a "secret recipe" filling.

By the time everyone had compared cupcake fillings and Greg and Nicky had agreed to trade halves, I realized that my worries about whether Derek's two best friends would get along were groundless. They were doing just fine.

In fact, if anything, it was Derek who was a little on the outside. He returned as we were reducing the last of the cupcakes to crumbs. He stood there for a moment, watching, like the host of a party who has somehow been left out.

And it wasn't Greg or Nicky who noticed him, but David Michael.

"Hey," he said. "I have some cupcake left. Want to share?" (David Michael is a terrific kid, if I do say so myself.)

Accepting David Michael's offer with a smile, Derek sat down and was soon part of the general conversation. But I couldn't help feeling a little sorry for him. He was on his way to being a truly famous film star, but underneath, he was a kid like any other. And no kid likes to work when he could be with his friends, which is exactly what Derek had to do.

By unanimous vote, the baby-sitters decided that a little after-lunch down time would be a good idea for everyone. We escorted the nine boys back to our sleeping car and saw them to their rooms with the promise of a trip to the club car (which Derek had assured us had some "outstanding cool games") later.

As soon as the boys were settled and we were back in our compartment, I turned to face Stacey and Abby. I could tell they were thinking what I was thinking:

MYSTERY.

"Who . . ." I began, then stopped as heavy footsteps pounded down the hall.

"Someone's in a hurry," remarked Abby.

Stacey sniffed. She sniffed again and leaped to her feet. "No wonder," she cried. "I smell smoke!"

We raced into the hall and looked up and down the corridor. It was empty. But black smoke was pouring from the far end.

"Get the kids out," Abby ordered. "I'll go knock on doors and warn anyone else who's here."

It seemed to take forever, but we shepherded the kids out into the corridor and away from the smoke, toward the doors at the other end. I could still hear Abby pounding on doors and shouting, "Come on! Come out! Fire!"

As Stacey, the boys, and I reached the doors, Abby and Ronald Pierce came charging up behind us. "That's everybody," Abby said, panting. "Let's get out of here."

I grabbed the handle of the door and pushed to slide it open. It didn't move.

I jerked on it, hard.

It didn't budge.

Smoke billowed around us. I heard someone coughing.

Stacey reached up and grabbed the door, and we both pulled as hard as we could.

But the door stayed closed.

"It won't open," I said with a gasp.

"Oh, no!" cried Mr. Pierce. "We're trapped!"

CHAPTER 5

Saturday

We may not be riding the Mystery Train to Charleston, but the Greenbrook Club is definitely not a bad place to put in some quality summer time. Posh but comfortable. Elegant yet simple. Okay, so maybe I'm getting a little carried away, but I do like the place. Who wouldn't?

Well, Stephen Stanton - Cha, the owner's son. I guess it is kind of hard on a kid to hang out in what is practically his mother's office.

The Greenbrook Club used to be called the Dark Woods Country Club, and it has a pretty dark history. It was incredibly discriminatory and exclusive. A lawsuit closed the club down for twenty years, until Nikki Stanton-Cha bought it and reopened it. Now it's welcoming instead of exclusionary, though it is still pretty elegant, just as Mal said.

Mal came prepared for work the first day that she, Jessi, Claud, and Mary Anne were scheduled to help open the club for the summer. She was prepared for sun, too. She wore a hat, a long-sleeved shirt, long baggy shorts, and sneakers with ankle socks. She had clipped sunshades onto her regular glasses, and she kept slathering SPF 30 sunscreen on as Jessi's dad drove her, Jessi, and Claudia to the entrance of the club.

Mary Anne, who lives within biking distance, was waiting by the front steps. She parked her bike and joined the other three as they walked up the stairs.

Both Mary Anne and Claudia were in cutoffs and sandals, with their swimming gear in their packs. Claudia was wearing a huge tie-dyed T-shirt knotted at the waist, and her sandals sported flowers that matched the flower barrette holding back her hair. Her gear was in a funky, bright yellow, plastic mesh tote that was exactly the same shade as the rims of her big, round sunglasses. Mary Anne was wearing a faded green Izod shirt and a baseball cap that read TED'S TOOLS. Jessi's hair was in a French braid. She was wearing blue bicycle shorts with a red cutoff T-shirt over a blue sports top and reef-runners.

Claudia glanced sideways at Mal. "That looks sort of like the bug-proof outfit you wore at Shadow Lake," she remarked. She was referring to a summer visit the BSC made to Watson's lakeside cabin in the mountains. Insects had swarmed around Mal there like, well, like bees to honey.

"At least I won't be fried by the sun," said Mal. Then she added, "You can use some of my sunscreen if you like."

"I brought some, too," said Jessi, patting her pack. "But it's only SPF fifteen."

Nikki Stanton-Cha was in the main dining area, pouring herself a cup of coffee. "Come on back," she called when she heard the front door open.

"Hi, Ms. Stanton-Cha," said Mary Anne politely.

"What is this?" she asked, smoothing back her blonde hair. "Last time you worked here, you called me Nikki, remember?"

Mary Anne looked a little abashed, but Claudia said cheerfully, "Hi, Nikki."

In addition to seeming younger than most moms, Nikki is very energetic and extremely strong-willed. How do we know this? Well, for one thing, she reopened the club against daunting odds, including a mystery that threatened to keep it closed until we helped solve it. For another, she stood up to her father, who didn't speak to her for ten years after he became angry with her for marrying Mr. Cha, who is from Korea.

Nikki looked around, called, "Stephen? Stephen!" and then turned back to us. "People will be arriving soon. I expect most of the action will center on the swimming pool. We have a lifeguard, of course, but during this opening weekend, you are going to act as counselors. You'll organize activities for the kids if they want that, keep an eye on things, even step in for some mini-baby-sitting if parents want to go for a snack, play a game of tennis, that sort of thing. I'll direct people to you as they arrive. . . . Stephen? Where . . . oh, good, there you are."

Nikki smiled as a boy with brown eyes and sandy brown hair — worn short except for a slightly longer tail in the back — appeared in the doorway. He was wearing jeans and a T-shirt.

"Hi," Stephen said shyly. Seven years old

and on the short side, Stephen did not resemble his mother very much in appearance or manner. He looked more like his father.

Mary Anne gave Stephen an encouraging smile. "Hi, Stephen."

Nikki said, "I thought you went to change into your swimsuit, Stephen."

He nodded, then shrugged. Finally he said, "The door was locked."

"To the boys' locker room? Oh, lord. The key's in the office . . ." Nikki marched briskly out of the room and returned a minute later to press a key into Mal's palm. "Unlock it for me, would you? Then you can all change and prepare for action." She grinned at us, walked out of the room, and turned at the door to throw her arms wide. "Let the summer begin!"

"Stephen! Hi, hi, hi!" called Karen as she led the charge of the Three Musketeers into the swimming area. Then she stopped and pointed dramatically to the signboard that listed the pool rules. "NO running around the pool," she said. Her best friends, Hannie Papadakis and Nancy Dawes, the other two Musketeers, stopped obediently.

Karen is not shy. She is also very, very strict about obeying rules. For example, she is the only member of the Krushers who has a shirt that spells Krushers with a *c* instead of a *k*. Why? Because she is obeying the rules of spelling.

Wearing the somewhat stunned look of a person who isn't used to Karen's high-octane energy, Stephen said, "Uh, hi, Karen."

Karen, Hannie, and Nancy walked along one side of the swimming pool to join Mal and Mary Anne. Mal was sitting in the shade of a beach umbrella. She had discarded her shirt and shorts in favor of a bathing suit, but she still had on her hat and dark glasses.

Mary Anne was in her bathing suit and her swim cap. Jackie Rodowsky and his brother Shea had just joined them, along with Ben Hobart, who is Mal's age.

In the shallow end of the pool, Claudia and Jessi were working with a group of younger kids that included four-year-old Jenny Prezzioso, Jamie Newton and Archie Rodowsky, who are also four, and Claire Pike. Claud and Jessi were helping them get used to the idea of putting their faces in the water all over again, something they hadn't tried since the summer before.

"HI, HI, HI," Karen said again in her loudest outdoor voice.

Hannie put her hands over her ears and Nancy giggled. Mary Anne couldn't help but smile, too. "Hi," she said.

"You guys are just in time. We're about to organize a game of freeze tag in the shallow end of the pool. Or maybe volleyball," Mal added, patting the brightly colored plastic ball next to her feet.

"Freeze tag!" Karen's blue eyes grew enormous behind her glasses. "Oh, no! The water is *freezing*! We're all going to be turned into enormous chunks of ice."

Smothering a laugh at Karen's runaway imagination, Mal said, "No, actually the water is fine."

Karen laughed, too. "I know," she said. She flung her towel down, whirled around, then walked quickly along the edge of the pool to where it wasn't so shallow. She leaped into the water, doubling her legs up for a cannonball.

"Wait for me," called Hannie. She cannonballed into the water after Karen. Nancy slithered in gingerly, making faces. Ben and Shea quickly followed Karen's and Hannie's suit, but Jackie got his feet tangled in the cutoffs he'd been wearing over his bathing suit as he tried to pull them off.

He hopped around wildly on one foot, then fell on top of Mal.

"Oof!" said Mal.

"Sorry," said Jackie.

"Better watch it," Mal warned him, "or I'll

huff and I'll puff and I'll *blow* you into the swimming pool."

With a shriek of fake fear, Jackie jumped up.

"You're not really going to throw us in the pool, are you?" asked Stephen.

"No way!" shouted Jackie.

"Wait," Stephen said to Jackie. "We could play cards. I have a new deck. It's called Old Bachelor."

"I've seen those cards," said Mal. "They're cool. We used to play the same game but we called it Old Maid. This is *much* better."

After a few more unsuccessful hops, Jackie escaped from his cutoffs and joined the others in the pool without further mishap.

Mary Anne climbed in, too. Mal threw her the ball.

"Come on," Ben called. "You're not chicken, are you?"

"No way!" said Mal, echoing Jackie. She stood up, took off her hat, slathered on some more lotion, and headed for the water.

Jackie waved at Stephen. "We'll play Old Bachelor later," he promised. "Come on in!"

Like Nancy, Stephen slid in, keeping a tight hold on the side. He pushed away from the edge and backed down the pool toward Claudia and Jessi until the water lapped around his waist.

Mary Anne tossed the ball into the air and

Shea leaped up to hit it, keeping it aloft as it came down. That was the whole game — simple but fun. Everyone swam and leaped and ducked and sputtered.

Then Mal noticed that instead of leaping up for the ball, Stephen seemed to be avoiding it. In fact, he seemed to be avoiding the game altogether.

Poor Stephen, thought Mal. Still shy, even though he's not the new kid in town anymore. She swatted the ball in his direction.

Stephen leaped for it, flailed wildly, then fell back into the water. He rose, spluttering and splashing, as the ball plopped down in front of him.

"Missed it, missed it," teased Ben. He scooped up the ball and offered it to Stephen to launch.

Stephen shook his head. He was still spluttering.

"Did you get water up your nose?" asked Jackie sympathetically. "That happens to me a lot. It'll go away."

Stephen nodded. But he also sloshed cautiously toward the shallowest part of the pool. "I'll just go sit on the steps for a minute. Until it feels better."

"You sure you're okay?" asked Mary Anne.

"Sure," said Stephen.

The play resumed. Stephen sat on the steps.

Although Ben and Jackie and the others called out to him to join them, he shook his head.

He stayed by the steps for most of the morning, and nothing anyone could say would persuade him to join in the games. Worried that Stephen wasn't feeling well, Mal sat down beside him.

"Hey," she said. "Come swim with us."

Stephen said, "Aren't you afraid of getting sunburned? It's awfully hot."

"You're right," said Mal. "No such thing as too much sunscreen. You want me to put some on your back for you?"

"Okay," said Stephen.

As Mal was spreading sunscreen on Stephen's shoulders, Jenny Prezzioso joined them.

"I'm tired of sticking my face in the water," she complained. "I don't want to get my hair wet."

"You have a bathing cap on," said Mal. "I don't think you need to worry."

"I don't want to get my cap wet, either," answered Jenny. "It's new."

Jenny is very neat and fussy about what she wears. Her pale green swimming cap with the ruffled edge matched her splash print pale green and pink tank suit. So Mal wasn't surprised by Jenny's statement.

She just nodded.

"We could play Old Bachelor," suggested

Stephen. "Then you wouldn't have to go back in the water."

"Okay," said Jenny happily, plopping down on the towel beneath the umbrella. "You want to play, too?" she asked Mal.

Mal looked at the sun. She looked at her bottle of sunscreen. She looked at Stephen and discovered he was watching her anxiously. "Okay," she said. "Why not?"

So Mal and Jenny and Stephen played Old Bachelor until lunchtime.

It was fun and she enjoyed herself, but she couldn't help wondering what was going on with Stephen.

It's a mystery, she thought and smiled to herself. She'd put that in the BSC notebook so everyone could read it when they got back.

CHAPTER 6

This is a stupid way to die, I thought, almost calmly.

"Move!" shouted Mr. Pierce and flung himself at the door again. He staggered back. The door didn't budge.

The smoke grew thicker. I grabbed the handle, half-expecting it to be hot from the fire. But it was cool — and unyielding.

"Get down," I heard Abby order the kids. "You can breathe better if you get down."

My eyes were stinging. I was taking shallow breaths and trying not to choke. I grabbed the door handle again and yanked hard.

The handle moved in my hand. Then the door slipped open so suddenly that I fell right through it.

I'm not sure, but I think Mr. Pierce stepped on me as he charged through with his son under one arm.

Then I was being helped to my feet and

we were hustling along the corridor. We were staying in the first in the line of sleeping cars, which were arranged in order of importance, with the big stars and big shots in the back of the train for security and privacy. As conductors and staff charged by I vaguely wondered if the fire had started in one of those cars.

Then I heard someone say, "It's a smoke bomb," in a tone of profound disgust.

I recovered my senses at that. "A smoke bomb?" I said. I was outraged. "Who would do a majorly stupid thing like that? What dimwit would put a smoke bomb on a train?"

A conductor glanced at me.

David Michael said, "Ow!"

I looked down and realized that I was gripping his shoulder way too tightly.

"Sorry," I said, making my voice calmer.

Stacey said, "Why don't we go down to the club car while they clean this mess up. I don't think we can do much here."

"All right," I said. "After all, it was only a smoke bomb."

Linny laughed. "I'm glad it wasn't a *stink* bomb."

That made all the boys go off in gales of laughter. Relieved that they were recovering so quickly, I forced myself to smile as I followed them down the corridor.

Suddenly I stopped and turned to the conductor. "A smoke bomb?" I said.

He nodded. "At the other end of your sleeping car, just inside the door."

"Whoever did it also locked the door so we couldn't get out. What was the point of this joke — to scare us to death?" I said.

"I don't know," said the conductor, looking worried. "But whoever locked your door had to have had a key. That's the only way the doors can be locked from either side."

"A key? Who on this train has keys?" I asked quickly.

The conductor shrugged. "We keep a master set on a latch inside a supply closet in the staff quarters," he said. "And of course all of the conductors have keys. So do a lot of the other staff." He shrugged again. "It could have been almost anybody."

"So Rock Harding was *locked out* of the editing room. *Reeltime* magazine said that it was because his last few movies were duds and the producers of this movie didn't want to take any chances. So Rock will do *anything* it takes to make sure this flick flies, because if it tanks, then he'll never eat lunch in Hollywood again."

It was a little after seven-thirty and we'd just finished dinner. Stacey was filling me in on

Rock Harding, the director of *Night Train to Charleston*. I'd already heard about "Atlantic's Antics," the gossip column Jane Atlantic wrote for the *New York Arrow*, and how most of Hollywood hated and feared her. She supposedly knew all kinds of secrets about the rich and famous, which was the reason that she was the only reporter permitted actually to stay on board the Mystery Train for the whole trip, and in her own compartment in one of the sleeping cars, while the other reporters were allowed to board only for short rides or to pick up interviews and photo opportunities at prearranged stops along the way. I'd also heard about Mr. Pierce's big break, selling the script of *Night Train* after years of teaching. *And* more about Benjamin Athens' habit of trashing hotel rooms. He apparently thought it was all a big joke.

I wondered if smoke bombs fell into the same category for him.

We weren't just gossiping. We were trying to figure out who was behind the increasingly nasty incidents that were plaguing the train. Rock, who would do anything to make his movie a success? Did he think of rubber hands and smoke bombs and anonymous threats as good publicity stunts? Or was Anne Arbour being overzealous in her job as publicist? Were Rock and Anne in it together?

Maybe Jane had manufactured everything so she'd have scoops for her column. Maybe her antics weren't just confined to the printed page.

I heard shrieks and laughter coming from the middle of the club car and deduced that the game Abby was playing with Derek and his friends, which involved trying to flip a game piece into a little cup in the middle of the board before making a move, was not easy on a moving train, and was a perfect distraction. The boys, at least, seemed relatively unfazed by what was going on.

We were huddled in a window seat in one corner of the club car, taking a break from baby-sitting while Abby kept an eye on Derek and his friends. Since we *were* technically gossiping, we were naturally whispering. Maybe that's why we jumped about a mile when a voice from above us said, "Hello. You're Kristy, right? And . . . Stacey?"

"Uh, right," I said, hoping he hadn't overheard us — not that Mr. Pierce was a suspect. Unless he was a better actor than anyone else on the train, he'd been genuinely terrified when we'd been trapped in the sleeping car. "Hi, Mr. Pierce."

Mr. Pierce smiled. I was relieved. Clearly, he hadn't heard us. He looked, I thought, distracted, a little frazzled. Hanging onto one hand was Daniel, his son, and on the other was Todd Masters.

"I want more ice cream," said Daniel.

"You've had enough," his father said. Then added quickly to us, "Could you keep an eye on Daniel and Todd for an hour or so? I have an interview."

"Sure," said Stacey. She patted the seat next to her.

Todd sat down, and after a moment of mutinous glaring and scowling, Daniel sat down, too.

"Thanks," said Mr. Pierce fervently, as if we weren't just doing our job. "It's a big interview, a feature writer from *Screen Team*. You know, screenwriters almost never win any attention for the movies they write. At least, not like the stars, or the director. But what would they do without us?" He laughed nervously. "Mime?"

"Good luck," said Stacey.

"Good luck," I echoed.

After Mr. Pierce left, we studied our two reluctant charges. "So," I said. "What do you guys want to do? Besides eat ice cream, I mean."

Daniel scowled some more, but Todd said, "I want to go to the observation car."

"I wouldn't mind doing that myself," I said. On the observation car was a high dome made of panes of leaded glass, like a real observation car of the era in which the movie was set. The car was at the end of the train and had a platform for watching the stars.

I jumped up, the train swayed, and I waved my arms around. "Uh-oh," I cried. "Uh-ooooohhhh." I pretended to fall on top of Daniel.

That did it. His smile turned to giggles. "Silly," he said.

"I just hope I don't fall out of the observation car," I said.

"Maybe if Daniel holds your hand, you can keep your balance," said Stacey.

That did the trick. Soon a much happier Daniel was walking with Todd, Stacey, and me to the back of the train. Just as we reached the entrance of the observation car, the train swayed again, let out a long, melancholy whistle, and plunged into a tunnel.

The power went out.

"Oh!" gasped Daniel, and he clutched my hand more tightly.

"No sweat," I said cheerfully. "The power always goes out when the train goes into a tunnel, remember?"

"It'll come back on when we leave the tunnel," said Todd. "Right?"

"Right," said Stacey. "And the tunnel has lights in it, so we're not completely in the dark."

This was true. The lights of the tunnel flashed by in a dim strobe effect that brightened the car, then plunged us into the dark over and over again. It was pretty spooky, in my opinion, but I didn't say so.

Suddenly Daniel's grip tightened even more. "Do you hear someone?"

We fell silent. Then I heard a voice from the other end of the car. It sounded angry.

"Shhh," I hissed. Then I said, "Daniel, Todd, stay here. *Don't move.*"

Stacey and I crept quietly forward.

The voice grew louder. "You *cretin.* You're early. You shouldn't be on this train. *I* should be on this train."

The other figure neither moved nor spoke. Bright, dark, bright, the tunnel lights flashed by. The open door between the glassed-in area and the raised platform of the rear deck thumped rhythmically against the wall. The dark silhouettes of the two figures, swaying to the rhythm of the train, were erased and reappeared time and time again as the tunnel lights flashed by. We could hear much better than we could see.

The voice continued, rising hysterically. "I'm going to tell people the truth, do you hear me? The truth *you* can't live with!"

The shadows made everything seem to move. Did the silent figure turn? Did it step away? Or did it have a chance to move before the speaker screamed?

We plunged out of the tunnel. At the same moment the speaker suddenly seemed to rise in the air, out over the railing of the observation deck, and plunge down, down, down.

"No," Stacey whispered. "He just pushed that guy over the rail!"

I gasped as the second man turned. Was he going to come after us? Catch us? Push us out of the train, too?

My knees went weak. Automatically, I checked over my shoulder to see that Todd and Daniel were still safe.

The man ran forward, but along the outside walkway of the observation car.

The train whistled again.

Or was it the long, drawn-out scream of a dying man as he fell out of a train to his doom?

The whistle — or maybe it was the scream — stopped. And as the lights came on, I thought I heard a faraway splash in the water that glinted below the trestle we were passing over.

CHAPTER 7

Wₑ couldn't have stood there for more than a moment. Then we rushed forward to the observation platform. The protective railing was shoulder height on Stacey and much too narrow for anyone to slip through by accident.

Then something hit my legs, hard. I stifled a scream as I realized it was Daniel, followed by Todd.

"I want my dad," said Daniel, not quite hysterically.

Daniel's father, I thought wildly. What if it were Daniel's father who . . . no, it couldn't be.

But I found myself clutching Daniel's hand as hard as he was clutching mine.

We peered through the railing into the darkness. The glint of water was gone, and the train rushed off the bridge and into a curve.

"He's gone," Stacey said in a stunned voice.

"Help!" I screamed. "Help! Somebody help us! Man overboard!"

But who was going to hear us at the very back of the last car on the train?

Jane Atlantic, that's who. No wonder she knew so many secrets, I thought. Her hearing was excellent.

She burst into the observation car, ran to the deck, and stopped short when she saw us. "You," she said. "What's going on?"

I glanced at our two baby-sitting charges and said, "An accident. There's been an accident.

"A man," I continued, trying to remain calm. "A man went over the railing." I pointed with my shaking free hand.

Ms. Atlantic's eyes glittered strangely, I thought. But she said calmly, "Are you sure?"

"Yes," said Stacey. "We're sure."

Daniel suddenly wailed, "I want my daa-aad."

"I'll go find the conductor," said Stacey. Then she bolted from the observation car as if she couldn't stand being there another moment.

"What happened?" asked Ms. Atlantic.

I shook my head. I glanced down at Todd's and Daniel's pale, scared faces and tried to signal to Ms. Atlantic that she should wait to ask questions until they were gone.

"What were *you* doing here?" Ms. Atlantic demanded.

What an odd question. "Daniel and Todd wanted to look at the stars from the observation car," I said woodenly.

"The stars . . . oh," said Ms. Atlantic. She sounded disappointed.

Seeing my expression, she held up her hand. In it was a white piece of paper. "I guess you didn't send me this, then?"

"What is it?"

"A note. It says, 'If you want some real news, meet me in the observation car at eight PM sharp.' "

Just then, the train screeched to a halt, throwing us all off balance. By the time we regained our footing, the door at the far end of the car had banged open. I led Todd and Daniel down the steps and back into the interior of the car as Stacey and the conductor came to meet us. Behind them, Anne Arbour, Mr. Masters, and Mr. Pierce crowded forward. Mr. Masters scooped up Todd and Mr. Pierce knelt by Daniel.

"Anne, if this is some kind of publicity stunt . . ." began Mr. Masters. His eyes were angry, although he kept his face calm. Standing up, with Daniel in his arms, Mr. Pierce was pale and sweaty and breathing hard.

"It's not. I want to know what's going on here," she demanded.

"An accident," I said, looking at the two boys.

Mr. Pierce and Mr. Masters were quicker than Ms. Atlantic. They exchanged a look. Then Mr. Pierce said, "I'm going to put you two guys to bed. But hey, what about a little ice cream first?"

"Okay!" said Daniel. He looked a bit less scared.

"Me, too!" cried Todd.

"Me, three," said Mr. Pierce. "Let's go."

When they'd left, Stacey and I told our story. The conductor made us repeat it. Then Mr. Masters, Anne, and Ms. Atlantic peppered us with questions.

"It's impossible," said the conductor. "You'd have to have superhuman strength to lift an adult over that railing."

"I think the excitement has made your imaginations go overboard, not a passenger," Anne said to us.

"I know what I saw!" I cried.

"We're *not* making this up," Stacey said, almost shouting.

"If you said you saw someone go over, then I believe you," Mr. Masters interceded. He turned to the conductor. "The first thing to do is take a head count. See who's on the train."

The conductor's radio crackled to life. He listened, then said, "We're not quite in the middle of nowhere. The cops are here."

"This is going to ruin the schedule," Anne wailed. She scurried away to do damage control.

"Let it," said Jane Atlantic. I looked over and saw that excited glitter in her eyes. I also realized that in her hand she clutched her tape recorder, and that it was running.

An hour later, everyone, every single person on the train, had been accounted for. As Stacey and I sat in the club car, at the center of a group of accusing eyes, the police reported no signs of anyone in the water beneath the trestle near the tunnel. They assured us that they would continue to search, but it was plain that they didn't expect to find anyone.

When the police had left the train, Anne hissed at us, "Good going, kids."

I felt my face redden, and I saw Stacey's head jerk back as if she'd been slapped.

Jane Atlantic laughed. "Relax. All publicity is good publicity, right, sweetie?"

Anne turned on her heel and stalked away. Still smiling her unpleasant smile, Ms. Atlantic followed her.

"Kids," muttered Benjamin in disgust. I decided that he was an ugly jerk, no matter what the magazines said. And I was never going to see a single one of his movies.

Except this one, of course.

Mr. Masters put his hand on my shoulder. "Mistakes happen," he said. "Let's forget about it, shall we?"

Muttering and gesticulating, everyone gradually dispersed.

Abby said, "Next time you decide to witness a murder, could you wait until I'm around?"

"You do believe us, don't you?" asked Stacey.

"Of course I do," said Abby. "We just have to figure out how to prove it."

Abby's calm assumption that we were right and everybody else was wrong made me feel a little better.

"Evidence," I said. "We need evidence."

"Scene of the crime," said Abby.

"Right. I'll check it out now." I started to turn, then paused. "Stace? You coming?"

"I'll stay here and give Abby some help settling the kids down. They're kind of wound up."

"No kidding," I said. I slipped away and tried to act casual as I made my way back to the observation car.

It was empty. Somehow, that made me nervous. I had to force myself to examine every inch of the car, inside and out.

Nothing. *Nada.* A big, fat blank.

Until I reached the observation platform and

caught a glimpse of a white scrap of paper caught in the railing.

A clue, I thought. I bent forward and took it carefully between my thumb and forefinger to minimize the chance of messing up any incriminating fingerprints.

Then I saw what I'd found: a page from the script of *Night Train to Charleston*. Page 37, to be exact.

Was this a clue?

I looked up at the stars and thought hard. Were the nasty incidents and the threatening notes related to the crime I had witnessed? Was this some kind of extreme and horrible publicity stunt planned to promote a movie — or a star's career? Or was a jealous ex-husband behind it all? But I couldn't come up with any answers. Only more questions.

For instance, who was missing?

And why?

CHAPTER 8

Saturday

The pool rules, at least at the Greenbrook Club this summer. A little hot weather hasn't hurt, of course. But not everybody has been enjoying the opening of the club. Take Stephen, for example. He was like a fish out of water with the other kids. At first I thought it was his shyness. Then I found out the real reason.

"I saw a movie," said Karen. "It was about a party at a beach. It had a beautiful lifeguard and a handsome surfer and there was this monster — "

"A beach party," Jessi said quickly. "Now, that sounds like fun."

Hannie said, "I wish we could have a beach party."

Glancing toward the lifeguard who had appeared for the afternoon shift, and who was as good-looking as the lifeguard who'd worked the morning shift, Claudia said, "Well, we have the lifeguard. All we need is the beach."

To celebrate the opening of the Greenbrook summer season, Nikki had laid out a scrumptious lunch for the adults in the more formal dining room, while the kids had been given free hot dogs, hamburgers, and pizza in the snack bar. The pool had been closed to prevent anyone from being tempted to go swimming too soon after eating.

Now a large group of kids had gathered around the edge of the pool. The Three Musketeers were back, along with Jackie; Ben; Stephen; Jessi's sister, Becca; Charlotte Johanssen; Luke Martinez; and the same group of four- and five-year-olds who had been practicing swimming earlier. They were all dangling their feet in the water, kicking impatiently and watching the large clock by the entrance to the snack bar. It wasn't quite time for the pool to reopen.

"We could go play in the maze," Stephen suggested. He was referring to a real maze, with old-fashioned high hedge walls and fake exits and dead ends that stood on the grounds of the club. "We could play hide-and-seek."

"It's too hot to run," said Becca. "And I haven't even been in the pool yet."

"Me, neither," agreed Charlotte. "We'd roast in the sun."

"If I roasted, I'd puke for sure," Ben said.

"Eeeeewwww," shrieked Nancy.

"Ick," cried Hannie.

Luke, Ben, and Jackie immediately began to make gagging, barfing noises, which made the Three Musketeers shriek even more.

At the suggestion that someone might puke, Jenny had yanked her feet out of the pool and scooted backward until she was almost under the umbrella where Mal was enthroned, reapplying sunscreen.

"How about some more Old Bachelor?" Stephen said to Jenny. "You liked that."

Jessi looked over her shoulder and realized that Stephen was the only one, except Mal and now Jenny, who wasn't poised on the edge of the pool, ready to plunge in the moment the lifeguard signaled them.

Stephen was sitting next to Mal. But he didn't need more sunscreen. Jessi knew that for sure because she had put some on him herself, right after lunch.

"Mal?" said Stephen.

"Thanks, Stephen. But I'm going to go swimming. Your mother just loaned me some new sunscreen. It has a protection factor of *sixty* and it's totally waterproof. I figure that should keep me from getting sunburned. Or from getting any more freckles."

Karen ceased shrieking abruptly to stare seriously at Mal. "If it's totally waterproof, how are you going to get it off? It could be stuck on you forever. You could turn all pale, like those things that live in caves and never go out in the sun. Then you'd shrivel up and — "

"Soap," said Mal. "It washes off with soap, I'm sure."

"But if it didn't, wouldn't that be *interesting*?" Karen asked.

"Very," said Mal dryly.

Mary Anne was staring at the lifeguard. Suddenly she said, "A party. We have the lifeguard, we have the water. We don't have the beach, but we do have a pool."

Instantly Jessi said, "A pool party. We could have a pool party."

"Excellent idea!" cried Claudia. "At night. So you wouldn't have to worry about sunburn, Mal. And the pool has lights, and we could string lanterns around the pool."

"And have races," cried Ben.

"Games," suggested Luke. "Lots of games."

"With prizes," added Charlotte.

The idea was an instant success. The kids peppered the four baby-sitters with suggestions. Finally, Jessi said, "Wait. First things first. We have to clear it with Nikki and figure out a good time — "

"I don't think pool parties are allowed," said Stephen suddenly.

A disappointed silence fell. Jessi studied Stephen. He wasn't looking at anybody. He was staring down at his feet. It was the posture of someone who isn't quite telling the truth.

"You don't think pool parties are allowed?" she said gently. "But you're not sure."

Stephen shrugged.

Mary Anne jumped to her feet. "There's only one way to find out. I'll go ask."

Of course, pool parties were allowed. When Mary Anne returned a few minutes later and gave us all a thumbs-up as she walked (not ran) to us, everyone burst into noisy cheers.

"She thinks the day after tomorrow might

work," Mary Anne said. "That'll give us time to plan it, and she'll make arrangements for a lifeguard to be on duty."

"Excellent," said Jessi, glancing toward the guy on the stand.

The party plans were in full swing when the lifeguard blew the whistle. But that didn't stop the entire group of kids from hurling themselves into the water when they heard it. A sheet of water went up like a tidal wave.

Even Mal, who was still under her umbrella, got drenched. Claudia, who had stayed by the steps with the beginners, burst out laughing.

So did everyone else.

Everyone except Stephen. As Mal stood up and headed for the pool, saying, "I guess I won't have to get used to the water," Stephen rose slowly.

"I'll go find a towel," he said.

"Just come on in the water," said Jessi.

Stephen shook his head. He turned away.

Impulsively, Jessi hoisted herself out of the pool and followed him.

"I can do it myself," said Stephen. "I'm not a baby."

"I know that. I just thought you might like some company," said Jessi.

"I may not come back to the pool right away," said Stephen. He stopped at the side of the clubhouse.

"Where are you thinking of going?"

He shrugged. "I don't know. Maybe I'll go hit some tennis balls."

"By yourself?"

He shrugged again. Then he said, "Unless you want to come with me." He glanced hopefully at Jessi.

"I'm not much of a tennis player, and it's the hottest time of the day," Jessi replied. Then she said, "Don't you want to play in the pool with us?"

Stephen stopped. He lowered his head to stare at his feet again.

Jessi stopped, too. But she didn't say anything. She waited.

"I-I can't," Stephen said, so softly Jessi almost couldn't hear him.

Jessi kept quiet.

Stephen burst out, "I *can't*! I can't. I can't."

"You can't play in the pool with us?"

Putting his hand up over his mouth, as if he'd like to catch the words even as he spoke them, Stephen said very, very softly, "I can't swim. I try and try and I keep sinking. I'm afraid I'll drown."

So that was it.

Stephen took his hand down from his mouth and looked at Jessi with panicked eyes. "You won't tell, will you? I don't want them to laugh at me!"

"No one's going to laugh at you," said Jessi.

"Yes, they will. And then they won't be friends with me," Stephen said. He looked as if he were about to cry.

Gently, Jessi laid one hand on his shoulder. "I won't tell. And they'll never find out. Because I'm going to give you one of my super-duper special secret swimming lessons."

"Secret?"

Lowering her voice and leaning forward, Jessi said, "Meet me by the pool steps at five forty-five after everyone has left. Deal?" She held out her hand.

Stephen shrugged. But he held out his hand and shook hers. "Deal," he whispered.

At 5:47, Stephen was hip-deep on the bottom step at the shallow end of the pool. Jessi handed him a kickboard. "Rest the upper half of your body on this," she said. "And kick across the pool next to the wall here. You can't sink because you have the kickboard. If you get scared, just put your feet down."

Stephen got scared, several times. But with Jessi's encouragement, he kept going.

At 6:01, he'd made it across without once putting his feet down.

He looked more hopeful. He did it again. And again. And again.

He did it so many times that it became easy — and a little boring.

At 6:15 he said, "I want to try something else."

"Okay," said Jessi.

By the time the lesson was over, Stephen had managed to dog-paddle across the shallow end, next to the wall. Then Jessi showed him how to sink to the bottom of the shallow end and hold his breath.

He floated to the top, every time.

"When you fill up your lungs with air," Jessi explained, "it's like turning yourself into a big beach ball. And beach balls never stay underwater."

"Cool," said Stephen.

He'd clearly had lessons before. But somehow he'd just never been able to put together everything he'd learned.

At 6:45, Jessi said, "We have to go."

"Will you give me another secret lesson? Tomorrow?" Stephen asked.

"You bet," said Jessi. "And you know what? If I give you two more secret lessons, I think you'll be able to swim with everyone at the pool party."

Stephen thought about this. Then he nodded and grinned. "Me, too," he said.

CHAPTER 9

Abby said it and it's her worst pun yet, but it's true — there's an ocean of mystery about Jane Atlantic, which is why I decided I should keep an eye on her.

For one thing, I wasn't sure I believed her story about receiving a note to meet someone at the observation car. Maybe she had, maybe she hadn't. Maybe she'd written the note herself. Maybe she'd written *all* the notes — including the ones in our programs — herself, to stir up a good story.

But why would she throw someone from the train? And if she had, how could she have returned to the sleeping car so calmly? She hadn't even been breathing hard.

Everyone had been allowed to stay up late, and Derek had had to stay up *extra* late to do some publicity at the last scheduled stop for the evening. "I'm *so* sorry, Derek," Anne said as she shepherded him out of the sleeping car, where everyone else was getting ready for bed. "But we're running late." She shot me a mean look. I glared back at her.

I definitely didn't like Anne now as much as I first had.

Beside me, Abby murmured, "Didn't someone say any publicity is good publicity? I think I'm going to keep an eye on her."

I whispered, "I think we all need to do a little post-bedtime detective work."

"Whatever you say, Agatha Kristy," Abby replied, grinning, and I groaned.

After everyone was in bed — including Derek — we'd had a quick emergency meeting with Stacey and agreed to get up extra early to search for clues. "Anne could be doing all this for publicity," I said. "Or she and Rock could be in it together."

Stacey said, "Publicity stunts are one thing. But murder is a little extreme."

"What about Elle's ex, the stuntman?" asked Abby. "*He's* got some major motivation. Or Jane — she could have staged the whole thing."

True enough, I thought. Maybe that's why she'd been so calm afterward. She'd had it all planned. We had plenty of suspects, but not enough clues.

Which is why, while almost everyone else on the train was still in bed, I was in the dining car.

Earlier, Jane had commandeered a booth in one corner of the car, where she could keep an eye on everyone who came and went. To make it clear that this was *her* place and no one else's, she'd spread out paper and pens and even left her laptop on the white tablecloth in front of her place, turning the booth into a sort of makeshift office. But she wasn't there now.

I slid into the booth and sorted through the

papers. And I found the note slid beneath Jane's laptop: IF YOU WANT SOME REAL NEWS, MEET ME IN THE OBSERVATION CAR AT 8 PM SHARP. DON'T BE LATE.

So she *had* received a note, I thought. A note typed exactly as all the other notes had been typed, on a small sheet of white paper.

The laptop was still on, plugged into a special outlet and attached, I noted, to what looked like some kind of phone wire. Ms. Atlantic was ready to send a hot story in at a moment's notice. If it was on, she was up already, and using it. She could return at *any* moment.

Quickly, I touched a button and the screen saver, an *Arrow* logo, disappeared. I found myself staring at a schedule. I scanned it and saw that Ms. Atlantic's appointments for the previous day did *not* include any kind of a meeting between seven and nine P.M.

No alibi. Not that writing someone on your schedule is a good alibi.

I stared at the screen. Maybe, I thought, Ms. Atlantic hadn't received the note after all. Maybe *she* had sent it to the victim, and then grabbed it back after pushing him off the observation deck. She could have typed this note, and all the others, if her laptop had one of those built-in printers.

I heard the sound of cutlery being sorted from the far end of the car and realized that the staff was about to start putting out place settings for breakfast. I leaped to my feet and made myself scarce.

Sunday

No one in Hollywood has real names, and I don't think Anne Arbour's is real. In fact, it sounds like one of my bad puns. But just because you have a phony name doesn't mean that you murdered someone. Does it?

Abby was ready and waiting when Anne Arbour slipped out of her sleeping compartment that morning. Anne might have been an early riser, but Abby was earlier. She shadowed Anne to the club car.

In a grumpy voice Anne demanded coffee, then slumped down over the cup. After a moment, she took out her pocket organizer and began to punch things into it.

Abby asked for orange juice and smiled innocently at the publicist while she waited.

Ms. Arbour frowned.

This helped. Abby didn't feel so bad about what she planned to do next.

She returned to the sleeping car and slipped into Anne's room. She was surprised to find the door unlocked — until she saw Anne's room.

The first big discovery? Anne Arbour was a major mess maker. Clothes, shoes, makeup, and papers were carelessly scattered everywhere. So it wasn't surprising that she would forget to lock her door. After recovering from the shock, Abby decided that although the chaos would make checking out her room difficult, it would also mean that Arbour probably couldn't tell if anyone had been there. So she didn't use a lot of caution as she sifted through the debris.

Abby then discovered that Anne was a compulsive list maker. Every scrap of paper seemed to be covered with lists: She found two packing lists, a list of books to read, a list of emergency phone numbers, a list of important birthdays, a list of names that I *think* were pet names (Bowers? Spotto? Whiskerkins?), and a list of stocks. She also turned up a coffee-stained copy of the script with the word FINAL stamped on the cover in black, and, finally, a printed timetable.

Abby reasoned that since Anne spent valuable time logging things into her handheld organizer, she could be careless with these other lists because they were just backup.

The last list Abby found was actually not on the floor but wedged under a bottle of perfume on the edge of the sink. It was a list of guests on the train. It had a row of checks on it — and everybody was present and accounted for except one person. A reporter from New Jersey had been scratched off. In parentheses a note read, "Missed train!!!!"

Other names were of reporters who had been granted "travel privileges." They had been allowed to board at various points and ride the Mystery Train to conduct interviews and so forth, until reaching the next stop. But each reporter was checked off for both boarding and departure points.

Jane Atlantic was the only reporter allowed on in Boston and scheduled not to depart until everyone else did, in Charleston.

Abby frowned as ferociously as Arbour had earlier.

Everyone was present and accounted for.

Who had gone overboard? And where had the person come from? Was there — had there been — a stowaway on board?

Abby stuffed the list back where she had found it and went back out into the corridor, more mystified than ever.

Sunday

What do movie stars do early in the morning? They eat breakfast. They do this by having it sent to their compartments. When I discovered this, I thought I'd come up with a pretty good plan to keep an eye on Benjamin and Elle.

A voice growled, "Leave it, leave it, leave it, willya?" The waiter didn't knock again. He set the silver-domed tray down, lifted the lid briefly (to make sure it was just fruit, eggs, toast, bacon, and coffee, with no body parts), then walked away.

Stacey leaped to the door, picked up the tray, and knocked softly again.

"All *right*," the voice grumbled.

Benjamin Athens opened his door. He did not look good in the morning. He had a heavy beard, bags under his eyes, and — Stacey took a step back — bad breath.

"Sleep well, sir?" Stacey asked, trying to sound like a waiter.

She needn't have bothered with the disguise. Benjamin said, "No. Trains make me seasick." He took the tray, shoved a quarter into her hand, and closed the door.

Stace looked at the quarter. A quarter? A

quarter from a rich, famous guy like Benjamin?

"Thanks," she said, loudly and sarcastically. She shoved the quarter in her pocket and wondered if Elle knew what a cheap creep Benjamin was.

Elle answered the door promptly when the waiter returned with her food. She looked very pulled together though sleepy. She yawned. "If this is Washington, it must be Sunday, right?" she said. She slipped something into the waiter's hand that made him stammer, "Th-thanks Ms. San Carlos!"

Just Stacey's luck. She'd chosen the cheap tipper. She watched in disgust as the waiter walked away. Elle had slept well and Benjamin had slept badly. So his sleeplessness couldn't be blamed on any fight the two might have had. For a moment Stacey wondered if Elle's husband could have secretly boarded the train. Maybe he had, and had lured Benjamin to the platform car, and *Benjamin* had thrown Charlie off. Maybe that's why Benjamin looked so harried. Guilt was preventing him from sleeping.

But that theory was ruined a moment later when a conductor knocked on Elle's door. "Telegram," he said.

She opened the door, grinned ruefully at the conductor, and said, "Oh, dear. Another one?"

"Yes, Ms. San Carlos."

"Let me guess. Charlie's still pining away for me in Boston. This telegram is just to let me know. See? I was right! How many telegrams has he sent since we left? Fourteen? Poor Charlie. He never was very good at investing his money wisely."

The door closed and Stacey realized that it had also closed on the possibility that Charlie was on board the train. If he had sent fourteen telegrams since the previous afternoon, no way could he have been on board and then thrown over by Ben.

Unless, she thought, he'd arranged for someone to send the telegrams beforehand, to cover himself while he stalked Benjamin. Hm-mmm . . .

"Ms. Atlantic? Ms. Atlantic!" A hand fell on Stacey's shoulder. Stacey turned as the voice went on. "Ms. Atlantic, we were wondering if . . . Oh! Sorry."

One of the assistants had mistaken Stacey for Jane Atlantic, at least from behind.

"No problem," said Stacey, flattered. She turned to head back to her compartment. At least she'd sort of ruled out a possible suspect, but the murder on the Mystery Train was still as big a mystery as ever.

CHAPTER 10

The Brunch on Board stop of the Mystery Train, in Washington, D.C., lasted for hours. The train stayed in the station, and people disembarked to go to a fancy restaurant while the crew brought important things on board, such as more fresh flowers for the compartments in which the stars were staying.

Derek did his usual admirable job of talking to reporters and posing for photographs, but his father gave him permission to skip the brunch (despite dark looks from Anne).

She managed to recoup this publicity loss, however, by telling the reporters all about Derek's "nice, normal little friends," and herding Greg, James, David Michael, Buddy, Linny, and Nicky front and center to be photographed.

"Aren't they sweet?" she kept saying.

The boys took it with good grace. In fact, although the Stoneybrook kids tried to act cool, I think they were kind of excited about the prospect of having their photograph in the news.

Todd and Daniel, to my surprise, had elected to go to the brunch with Mr. Masters and Daniel's father. Maybe they'd been promised ice cream for dessert.

As soon as all the star power had left the train, we got down to business. After making the boys promise not to alarm Todd and Daniel with the information, we filled them in on what had happened and what our detective work had turned up so far: nothing.

"Not nothing," said Nicky. "You have the page from the script."

"Score one for Nickman!" said Greg. He thumped Nicky on the shoulder and Nicky gave him a friendly shove back. In Derek's frequent absences to do publicity work for the movie, Greg and Nicky had bonded big time.

In fact, they seemed to have squeezed Derek out of the loop altogether. I saw Derek glance from one to the other and I thought he looked unhappy.

"I think Charlie did it," said Linny. "I bet he paid someone to send Elle all those telegrams so he'd have an alibi!"

"Yeah!" Buddy.

"Yeah, but who did Charlie push over the side?" asked David Michael.

"What I want to know is, what does one torn piece of script mean?" asked Stacey.

Abby said, "Maybe it doesn't mean anything. We don't have much else to go on."

Greg said, "It had to come from someone's script, didn't it?"

"You're right!" exclaimed Derek.

"But who has scripts?" I asked. "I mean, the movie's finished. Why would they carry the script around?"

Derek said, "Lots of people keep theirs, just to see how the movie compares to the script. For instance, some scenes that are in the script are taken out after they're shot, and things like that. I know that Anne put a copy of the script in each of the VIP compartments on this trip."

We hadn't had a copy of the script in our room. I guess Anne hadn't thought we were Very Important Persons. In fact, at the moment, I suspected she would label us VBPs — Very Big Pains.

Well, she was going to be BTS — Big Time Sorry — when we solved the mystery.

We went on a script hunt. This was both easier and harder than it sounds. Easy, because no one had locked his door. In fact, many of the compartments just had their curtains drawn across the entries. People on this train were incredibly trusting. Easier still, because having Derek with us gave us the run of the train.

Harder, because with so many scripts and so many people, we couldn't be sure of finding them all. Still, it was worth a try.

We found Rock Harding's with no problem. His compartment looked as if he didn't even sleep there. The script was in the outside pocket of a soft-sided briefcase on the floor of his closet. It was fresh and new-looking and had SOUVENIR COPY stamped on it.

"Those are the ones Jane handed out," said Derek. He reached down into the briefcase and brought out another copy of the script, heavily creased and rumpled, with a rainbow of colored pages in it. But both scripts were complete.

Elle's compartment was filled with flowers. Her closet was crammed with clothes.

Even Stacey was stunned. "When does she find time to wear all these things? I'd still be unpacking."

"She has a personal assistant for that," said Derek.

"Her personal assistant isn't still around is she?" I asked quickly.

"Nope. Elle sent her to look for a few things she needed," Derek reported.

"Like what?" Abby snorted. "She doesn't have a single spare inch of space, and this compartment is enormous."

David Michael sneezed. He sneezed again.

"Shh," I said automatically.

"ACHOO!"

"It's the flowers," Abby said, her own nose wrinkling. "If I stay in here another second, I'm going to have an allergy attack. Come on, David Michael, let's keep watch in the corridor."

Elle's script was the publicity copy, every neat page in place.

"I guess she didn't have room for more than one script," said Linny.

Benjamin's closet was as packed with clothes as Elle's. He'd also brought an extra mirror, which was hung on the back of the compartment door. Fortunately, his flowers were limited to one bouquet, so Abby and David Michael could rejoin us.

"We'll keep watch," said Greg. "Come on, Nicky."

"I'll come, too," said Derek.

"That's okay. Two people are enough," said Greg.

Derek opened his mouth to say something, then closed it. He definitely looked hurt.

The only "important" discovery was made by James. "The guy wears perfume!" he said, coming out of the bathroom.

"Lots of guys do," said Abby.

"I wouldn't! Not even to be a screen star!" James said vehemently.

"You might change your mind," Stacey told him. "I like perfume on guys sometimes."

"No way!" declared James, and the others nodded emphatically.

We couldn't help but laugh, even though we found only the publicity script, still in its fancy envelope, tossed in the top drawer of Benjamin's traveling trunk.

The rest of our search was no more successful. Every script we could find was intact.

Feeling discouraged, we went back to our compartment. When everyone returned from brunch, the train got underway again.

We spent the afternoon making publicity stops (including another lengthy layover in Richmond, Virginia). Derek made the interview rounds and, along with the other stars, acted out a scene from the movie for several reporters and the rest of us. Everyone applauded, and the reporters crowded around him again afterward.

I couldn't help but notice how he seemed to be glancing our way, mainly toward Nicky and Greg.

Abby noticed it, too. "He feels left out," she said. "Particularly by Nicky and Greg. I don't think they're ignoring him deliberately. But he's so busy that they've just gotten into the habit of not including him."

We pulled out of Richmond late in the afternoon. After that, we made one more stop. When the train was finally in motion again, Derek joined us in the club car, sliding in next to Linny.

"You must be tired," Abby said.

Derek smiled a bit wanly. "I am, I think."

"Hard work," said Greg.

"Yeah," said Derek. Then he said, "I forgot. They've made a board game of the movie. My dad has an early copy of it, and he said we could borrow it and try it out if we wanted."

"Super," said Nicky.

Derek brightened a little.

"It'll be nice for you to spend some time with us. I know you've wanted to, but you've had to work," I said pointedly.

"Wow," said Linny. "You've had to work practically the whole time, haven't you? That's no fun."

I saw Nicky look thoughtful, and I silently cheered Linny.

"Yeah, I *have* missed goofing with you guys." He brightened, looked around, and lowered his voice. "But it's been fun looking for clues to solve the mystery."

Just then, Anne hurried to us and put her hand on Derek's arm. "Derek," she said. "The reporter from *Screen Team* has a few questions."

Derek looked unhappy but he stood up.

"Bummer," said Nicky.

"Yeah," said Greg. "Hurry back."

Derek brightened. "Yeah?"

"Definitely!" said Nicky.

Derek the kid looked a lot happier as he left to be Derek the star.

We set up the game after dinner. Derek's character was one of the pieces, which made everybody laugh. James said that his piece, the Ben character, smelled like perfume. All the boys thought this was hugely funny. Stacey and Abby and I rolled our eyes.

Then, in midgame, I stopped. "Wait a minute," I said.

I pulled the piece of script from my pocket carefully, glanced around the room, then slid it across to Derek. "Read this."

He did. He looked up. "This isn't the right script," he said.

"I *thought* the characters' names weren't right," I said.

"No, they're not. Not a single character's name is the same. No one in the movie has these names, but some of the lines are the same."

"Do you think it's a fake script?" Abby asked.

"Maybe," said Stacey. "But why? How could that affect anyone on the train?"

I didn't know. So I brooded. And brooded. I

brooded all through the game. I brooded as we put the kids to bed.

Stacey and Abby decided to go to the club car.

I sat on my bed and brooded some more.

And then, as I stared at that scrap of paper, it hit me.

I leaped to my feet. I ran to the door and out into the corridor. I had to find Stacey and Abby. I had to —

The train lurched. It bucked like a wild horse. I reeled from one wall to the other and wondered if we were about to go off the tracks. The train seemed to pick up speed — and so did my heart.

Then the lights went out.

CHAPTER 11

Sunday

Party party, praty. We are real party anemals.
Pool party anemals.

Claudia had not only lit the pool area with lanterns, she'd also come up with another fantastic decorating idea. She'd persuaded Nikki to buy lots of brightly colored beach balls. Then she, Mary Anne, Jessi, and Mal had stenciled GREENBROOK CLUB POOL PARTY KID on each one.

The kids arrived at the party to find the pool filled with the balls.

Naturally, this was a big hit.

After they'd worked off some of their energy with swimming and splashing, Mal stood up and said, "Time for games. First, a cannonball contest. The winner will be the kid who makes the biggest cannonball splash. Judges, to your places."

The Three Musketeers had volunteered to be judges. They sat in chairs (well back from the splash zone) and held cards numbered from one to five. Mary Anne sat next to them, ready to write down the scores. The splash that earned the highest score would win.

When Jackie headed toward the edge of the pool for his turn, Karen flung down her card and cried, "WALK, DON'T RUN!"

Jackie stopped, wide-eyed, lost his balance, and fell in while everyone else cracked up.

His splash was tremendous.

After a hot debate among the judges, in part

because Karen said that his fall hadn't been a real cannonball, the prize went to Jackie and to Becca in a tie.

Stephen didn't win a prize, but he did jump in and made a very respectable splash.

For the younger kids, we had a face-in-the-water contest. We put weighted plastic dinosaur toys on the bottom of the shallowest part of the pool and let the kids bob down to grab them.

Greed soon overcame even Jenny's desire to avoid getting wet, and she emerged, clutching a purple stegosaurus and shouting, "I got one, I got one, I got one!"

The parents at poolside applauded and took many, many pictures.

But the biggest success of the evening was the silly bathing cap contest. Every single kid had gone all out for that one. As Claudia announced each entrant, Mary Anne, Jessi, and Mal made notes and tried not to laugh too hard. And every single kid enjoyed his or her moment in the spotlight to the fullest.

Karen strutted out like a model on the runway, her towel draped around her like a cape, wearing a bathing cap covered with sequins, beads, and every piece of old jewelry she could manage to attach. She'd even decorated a pair of sixties-style sunglasses and a pair of thongs to match. Hers was a real crowd pleaser.

Charlotte had made big basset hound ears for her swim cap. She demonstrated how the ears could be blown up like inner tubes. "It's a bathing cap and a safety device," she announced. "It'll help keep you afloat in an emergency!"

Ben had gone for gross. He was wearing a bathing cap with a jagged hole in one side. He'd painted red fingernail polish around the hole. He was wearing a whistle around his neck and holding a cardboard triangle. "I'm a lifeguard," he explained. "And this is all that's left of that shark that took a nip of my cap."

Claire Pike's entry was simpler but very funny. With Vanessa's help, she'd painted a face on the back of her cap. It was pretty funny to see Claire walking away from us — and see the painted face looking back at us as she retreated.

Other contestants included a camouflage cap, a rainbow cap, a fake pigtail swim cap, and even an invisible cap. It wasn't easy to decide among them.

In the end, Charlotte won first prize, Ben was awarded a prize for most original, and Karen and Claire tied for "reserve first prize."

Everyone applauded as the winners took one last turn around the pool.

Then it was time for more swimming. Greenbrook Club balls and kids' bodies went into motion, while the smell of the grills heating up for the cookout wafted through the air.

Claudia nudged Jessi and said, "Look."

By the pool steps, Stephen was talking solemnly to Claire and the four-year-olds. "Here," they heard him say. "If you hold your breath, you'll always float, you know. Just like one of these balls." He demonstrated.

Claire slid into the water and copied him. Soon the four littlest swimmers and Stephen were bobbing like corks.

"Good work," Claudia told Jessi.

"We all helped," said Jessi. "It was a team effort."

"But you figured it out first," Claudia said.

Now the parents were calling the younger kids, toweling them off, and helping them into dry clothes before dinner.

Mal rummaged around in her pack.

"Smells good," said Claudia, taking deep sniffs of the air. "Hot dogs."

"Turkey dogs, too," said Mary Anne. "And hamburgers."

"And make-your-own sundaes for dessert," said Claudia dreamily. "Junk food heaven: nuts, whipped cream, cherries, butterscotch topping, chocolate syrup, three kinds of ice cream."

"How do you know all that?" asked Jessi.

"I helped Nikki with the menu," Claudia

said simply and grinned. She took another deep sniff and frowned. "Ugh," she said. "I hope *that's* not on the menu."

"What?" Jessi sniffed and made a face.

Mary Anne said, "Smells — inedible. Smells like . . ."

The three girls turned. Mal was squirting something out of a bottle onto her arms.

She stopped as Jessi, Claudia, and Mary Anne stared at her.

"What?" she said. "What?"

"You don't need sunscreen, Mal. It's almost nighttime."

"It's BugBeDead," said Mal. "Insect repellent."

The girls stared at one another. Then they burst out laughing.

CHAPTER 12

I was *not* having fun. The train lurched one way and then another and I zigzagged down the corridor. I hit something hard with my shoulder, rebounded, and crunched my knee against something made of metal.

I couldn't see anything. I kept my hands out in front of me and smashed my knuckles against a knobby object. I tried to grab it to hold on to it, but another lurch of the speeding train sent me to my knees.

Just as I staggered to my feet, the train skidded to a stop with a long screech of brakes, and I was thrown into a backwards dive. I slid like an upended box turtle for several feet as the deafening screech went on and on.

Then my shoulder collided with — a wall?

I rolled over and hauled myself to my knees, and the train slammed to a stop. This time I was thrown forward onto my stomach.

"Oof," I gasped, the wind knocked out of me.

I lay there, taking slow deep breaths, and heard the intercom system crackle to life.

"Attention. Attention, all passengers. We are sorry for the inconvenience. We have experienced a slight temporary mechanical difficulty. We will be moving shortly."

Oh, no, I thought, *what now?* I had an idea that the "temporary mechanical difficulty" was no accident. Aloud, I said, "I'd settle for some light." Carefully, I rolled over and rose, unsteadily, to my feet.

The lights came on. I found I was at the far end of the sleeping car.

I staggered back to check on the boys. I started with Derek's compartment.

Naturally, they were awake *and* thought the whole thing had been totally cool. "My suitcase went sliding right across the floor!" announced Nicky happily.

"That's great," I said ironically.

"Totally excellent," agreed Greg.

"Well, stay put," I said. "It's getting late and we have a big day tomorrow."

Things were pretty much the same in David Michael's compartment. I went to look in on the little guys.

Todd and Daniel were in their pajamas, sitting cross-legged on Daniel's bed. They, too, seemed to think the incident had been an outstanding special effect. "We were playing pickup sticks," said Todd, "and they went *everywhere*. So now we're playing pickup sticks on the floor. Are you going to read to us?"

"No, not right now," I said. "Aren't you guys supposed to be asleep?"

"Abby said she'd come back and read to us before we went to sleep," Daniel said indignantly.

"Oh. Okay. She'll be here soon, then," I said. "In fact, I'm on my way to find her now."

Feeling bruised and battered and more than a little worried, I stepped back out into the corridor. It was empty. But something about that very emptiness made me uneasy.

Impulsively, I stuck my head back into Daniel's compartment. "Stay here," I ordered. "Don't go anywhere."

Daniel gave me another indignant look. "We're not *babies*."

"Right," I said.

I repeated my warning in the two compartments that Derek and the others were staying in. They were unimpressed by it, too.

"Kristy's kind of bossy sometimes," I heard David Michael explain as I left.

Most of the passengers on the train were

now in the stage car, I discovered, watching the reenactment of one of Ben and Elle's scenes. Things had reached a very dramatic point, so nobody noticed when I slipped in behind Stacey and Abby and leaned over to whisper in Stacey's ear. Stacey touched Abby's arm and they tiptoed out to join me in the dim corridor that led to the stage car.

Abby checked her watch and said, "Uh-oh. I promised Todd and Daniel I'd read them a bedtime story. I told them they didn't have to go to sleep until I did."

"Wait," I started to say. But at that instant a man with a mustache brushed by us, leaving the stage car. It looked as if the mustache was coming off. One of the actors in a bit part, I thought vaguely. The lurching of the train probably hadn't made it easy for him to apply his stage makeup.

"Catch you in a few," Abby said and hurried away before I could stop her.

"Kristy, what is it?" Stacey asked.

"I've solved the mystery, or at least part of it," I answered. I held up the scrap of script over which I'd been brooding. "Similar dialogue but different names, right? It's not a fake — it's a draft. The script was rewritten at least once. Remember, the other scripts were labeled 'Final.' That implies rewrites."

Stacey nodded vigorously. "Yes! And who would be carrying a first draft around? Someone like the screenwriter."

"Ronald Pierce," I said. "And on the night of the accident, he said he was going to an interview. But I saw Jane Atlantic's schedule. She didn't have an interview scheduled then, and she was the *only* reporter on the train."

"You're right," said Stacey. "And remember who Derek had an interview with this afternoon?"

"The reporter from *Screen Team*. And that's who Mr. Pierce claimed he was meeting. But the guy didn't even board the train until today!"

"So Ronald Pierce lied to us. Why?" mused Stacey. "Because he had something to hide. Like maybe a secret meeting on the observation deck."

"Now we just need to find out who he was meeting, and we'll know who he pushed overboard." A sudden chill ran down my spine. I'd just called Daniel's father a murderer.

"We have to tell someone now." Stacey's urgent voice interrupted my thoughts.

She was right. But . . . Ronald Pierce? He was weird, but then a lot of writers were probably weird. He had lied to us, but being a writer, being weird, even being a liar still didn't add up to being a murderer.

Did it?

"They're all in here. Come on," said Stacey.

Almost reluctantly, I followed her back into the stage car.

And stopped as the door closed behind me and my lungs filled with thick, black smoke.

CHAPTER 13

"Kristy!" Stacey shouted.

"Right behind you," I said with a gasp. I located her dimly outlined form and grabbed a handful of her shirt.

People were screaming. Smoke billowed through the air. Fortunately the lights hadn't gone out.

Keeping a firm hold on Stacey's shirt, I stepped back, opened the door, and propped it open.

"Stay calm, please. Everybody stay where you are and stay calm," I heard Mr. Masters call. "It's not a fire."

And even as he spoke, I could see that the smoke was lessening.

"Clear the vents," I heard someone else say.

Gradually, the smoke cleared. Through stinging eyes I saw people milling around.

A man I recognized as the physician's assistant on the train crew moved among the crowd, checking to make sure everyone was all right.

Mr. Masters was bending over one of the vents with Elle, while Benjamin and Mr. Harding pried at another one. Elle straightened up and said in a disgusted voice, "I thought so. Basic special effects. A smoke bomb set on a timer in the vent."

"Don't touch it," said Mr. Masters. "Maybe we can have it checked for fingerprints." His voice was grim and furious. "I don't know who is trying to sabotage this movie or why, but I'm going to find out."

I knew that had to be our big cue. I pulled Stacey forward from where we'd been standing in the doorway, taking big gulps of sweet, fresh air. "Mr. Masters," I said.

He turned.

Then someone screamed, "Oh, no! Look! The windows!"

That's when I saw it. The windows of the stage car were covered with ugly red letters, the same words over and over.

THE TRUTH WILL COME OUT! YOU CAN'T STOP ME! SAY GOOD-BYE TO WHAT YOU LOVE MOST!

"What does that mean?" said Jane Atlantic.

I thought I knew. I hoped I was wrong. I scanned the room, looking for Ronald Pierce. At last I located him. He was slumped in a chair, his head in his hands.

Stacey and I charged across the room, ignoring the babble of voices. "Mr. Pierce," I said in a low, urgent tone. "Mr. Pierce, we have to talk."

Mr. Pierce raised his head. His square glasses were smudged and his ruddy complexion was pale. He looked frightened and confused.

"Mr. Pierce," I said, my voice rising. "You have to tell us what is going on."

Heads turned. The babble of voices quieted. Stacey, Mr. Pierce, and I were suddenly center stage. My heart was pounding so hard I thought it would jump through my chest, but I knew that in front of all these witnesses, Mr. Pierce couldn't hurt us even if he was a murderer.

"Mr. Pierce," I said more loudly still, "WHAT IS GOING ON?"

He leaped to his feet. I choked down a scream and backed into Stacey as he grabbed my arm.

"Let her go!" cried Stacey, grabbing my other arm and pulling hard.

"No! No, you don't understand," said Mr. Pierce. He was so pale now that I thought he was going to faint. But his grip on my arm was insanely strong.

Insanely.

"Please let go of my arm," I said, trying to be polite to a possible maniac.

"It's Daniel," cried Mr. Pierce. "Oh, my lord, it's Daniel. He's going after Daniel. That's what he means by what I love most! I know it."

My knees grew weak and I was actually glad that two people were holding my arms in a death grip. Otherwise, I might have done something embarrassing myself, such as fall.

Then a surge of adrenaline pumped through me and I pulled my arm free of Mr. Pierce's. I turned.

"Wait!" he shrieked. "Stop! Where are you going?"

I didn't stop. There was no time to ask who "he" was. I began to run, pushing people out of my way, knocking over chairs, with Stacey right behind me.

"WAIT!" screamed Mr. Pierce. "Where are you going?"

"To find Daniel," I called over my shoulder as I ran to save Daniel's life.

CHAPTER 14

The train kept moving, swaying from side to side like a cradle, as if nothing could possibly be wrong.

"Abby," I panted. "She doesn't know."

"They'll be safe with Abby," I heard Stacey answer as she ran behind me. We raced on. We burst into the sleeping car and threw open the door of Daniel's compartment.

Abby looked up from the pickup sticks she'd been putting back into their box. "Hi! You won't believe what Todd and Daniel talked me into. A little game of hide-and-seek. Want to help me? . . . Kristy! Stacey! What's wrong?!"

Abby jumped up.

My mouth had gone dry. "We have to find them. Now! They're in terrible danger," I managed to say.

Mr. Pierce charged into the room, practically knocking me over. "Where is he?" he demanded hoarsely. "Where's Daniel?"

Abby didn't waste any time asking questions. "We'll find him," she said. "They can't have gone far."

Mr. Masters said, "We'll split up. That will make it faster."

Abby and Stacey hurried away to search. I went with Mr. Pierce. "Daniel!" I called. "Todd! Game's over! Come on out!"

"Daniel," shouted Mr. Pierce. *"Daniel!"*

"Try to sound calm," I told him. "Otherwise, you could scare him."

Mr. Pierce licked his lips. "You're right. Oh, this is all my fault. If only I hadn't . . . if only . . ."

"If only what?" I prompted as we yanked open bathroom and closet doors, looked under beds and behind suitcases.

"I based the idea for this screenplay on one submitted to me by a student years ago. Laurence Channing. . . . Daniel! Daniel, it's your dad. Come on out, son, so I can play, too. Daniel!"

We waited a moment, but no Daniel or Todd answered.

"Laurence Channing," I prompted, leaning over to look into a garbage receptacle.

"Laurence was furious when he found out. He wanted full credit for the screenplay I wrote. Of course, that was out of the question. Technically, I'd done nothing wrong . . ."

A technicality that might cost Daniel his life, I thought grimly, but I didn't say anything.

"Still, I paid him. And after I paid him the first time, he used it to blackmail me into paying him more. But even that wasn't enough. He began to make threats. He accused me of being in a conspiracy with everyone on the film to deprive him of the fame and money he deserved.

"I suspected he was behind the sabotage the moment it started. And I *knew* he was when I met him on the observation deck that night."

"So you pushed him from the train?" said Mr. Masters, who had come up behind us.

"No! No, it was a setup, don't you see? He'd planned it all to make me look like a murderer. But the only witnesses were two kids whom — "

" — nobody believed," finished Mr. Masters. He bent to look behind a suitcase and froze. "Todd?" he whispered.

"Rats," said Todd, uncurling. "You found me." Mr. Masters grabbed Todd so hard that Todd squeaked, "Ow, Dad."

"Sorry, son," said Mr. Masters. But he didn't let go of Todd's hand as we continued to search.

I suddenly remembered the note to Jane Atlantic. She'd missed her entrance cue, and ruined Laurence Channing's plans.

"He went into the water — and must have climbed back on board at the next stop. He must have had a car waiting."

"Daniel's not in this sleeping car," I announced. I reached for the door of the next one. We'd just stepped into it when Stacey and Abby entered the car from the other end. Abby pumped one fist in the air and stepped to one side to reveal . . .

"Daniel," cried Mr. Pierce in a ragged voice. "Son!"

"Hi, Daddy!" said Daniel. He started to run toward his father.

At the same moment, someone swooped out of one of the compartments.

In the fraction of a second before I launched myself forward, I saw blazing eyes and a mustache that was coming unglued.

The train rocked sideways and Channing was thrown off balance. I grabbed Daniel and rolled into one of the compartments. "Run!" I shouted to the others. "Run!"

I tried to slam the door of the compartment. Channing jammed his foot into the doorway. I stomped down hard and heard a howl of rage. I felt the door slipping from my fingers.

"Go into the bathroom and close the door," I said over my shoulder to Daniel. "Lock it."

"K-Kristy?" said Daniel.

"NOW!" I shouted.

He went. As the door slipped from my grasp, I heard the bathroom door close and lock.

Then Channing stood in front of me. He stepped forward, and I kicked him in the knee as hard as I could.

At the same moment, Ronald Pierce hit him from one side, knocking him to the floor of the corridor. I saw, or thought I saw, Abby and Stacey pile on.

Then I slammed the door of the compartment, locked it, and put my back against it. From outside I heard shouts and running footsteps.

Then silence.

Someone knocked on the door.

"Who is it?"

"Kristy?" said Abby's voice. "You can come out now."

"Are you sure?"

"It's okay, Kristy," said Mr. Masters. "We have him."

I heard someone making a snarling sound, like an animal.

Slowly I slid the door back.

Two conductors were lifting the struggling Channing from the floor. His arms had been tied behind his back with what looked like a pair of pants.

He raised his head and saw me standing in

the door. "You," he snarled. "If it hadn't been for you, I would have had justice."

"I wish I *had* pushed you off the train," said Mr. Pierce.

"You don't have the guts. I did it. I planned it all myself! Me! I'm the genius, not you."

They dragged him away. He was still screaming threats when the door closed behind him.

"Daniel's in the bathroom," I told Mr. Pierce.

He walked to the door. "Son," he said, "you can come out now."

The door opened and Daniel jumped out and threw his arms around his father's neck.

CHAPTER 15

"Charleston is hot!" complained Abby, fanning her face.

"But you have to admit, it's a cool-looking little town," said Stacey.

Abby and I burst out laughing. When Stacey looked puzzled, I said, "You thought Boston was a cute *little* town, too."

Stacey grinned.

We'd made it safely to Charleston. And in spite of all the delays — including an unplanned stop to deliver Laurence Channing into the arms of the police — we were almost on time. By noon we'd checked into our plush bed-and-breakfast inn overlooking the harbor. By one o'clock we were sitting in a horse-drawn carriage with Derek and his friends, taking a tour of one of the prettiest towns I had ever seen.

Todd was with us. Daniel was with Mr.

Pierce. I wondered if he would ever let Daniel out of his sight again.

"Charleston has been devastated by war, earthquake, flood, and hurricane," said our guide. "Many feel the adversity has only enriched her and made her more beautiful."

Did adversity enrich a person and make her more beautiful? Hmmm. I'd have to think about that. If it did, the events of the last few days meant I was going to be majorly enriched and drop-dead gorgeous.

That made me laugh. As if I were some nobrainer who thought looks were the only thing that mattered.

I should have been tired, but I wasn't. When we sent the boys to rest before getting ready for the premiere, I discovered that Stacey and Abby felt the same way. We headed for the front porch of the inn, which had a beautiful view of the water. Abby and I settled down to bounce gently on the long plank seat called a joggling board, while Stacey rocked to and fro in the swing. We didn't talk much. When we did, it was, of course, about the events aboard the Mystery Train.

"He never confessed to what he'd done," said Abby.

I knew she was talking about Mr. Pierce.

"When he told me, Mr. Masters heard him," I said. "He'll take care of it."

As if in answer to his name, Mr. Masters came out onto the porch.

"I just wanted to thank you," he said. "I'm sorry I ever doubted your word. What you did was incredibly brave, all of you, and especially you, Kristy."

"Hey, it's all in a day's work for the Baby-sitters Club," I said, embarrassed.

Mr. Masters smiled. "Maybe."

"What's going to happen to Mr. Channing?" asked Abby.

"And Mr. Pierce?" added Stacey.

"Mr. Channing has made a full confession. He knew more than enough about special effects and makeup to disguise himself and sneak on board the train. He'd traveled the route dozens of times before in recent months, always in disguise so no one would recognize him. But the police have found ticket stubs, among other things, in his apartment.

"He planned everything. Sent the notes, fiddled with the train controls so that it almost jumped the track, planted smoke bombs in the vents. And his plan almost succeeded."

"He thought Jane Atlantic would see the 'murder' and investigate. Her big scoop would be about how Ronald Pierce had stolen the screenplay — and murdered the real author," I said slowly.

Mr. Masters nodded. "He was going to let Ronald suffer through an arrest and trial, then come back after the sentencing and claim that he'd had amnesia from the fall. All along, he thought Ms. Atlantic had seen what happened. He'd mistaken you, Stacey, for her. That's when things began to go wrong for Channing."

"Wow," said Abby. "Cool. Good work, Stace."

Stacey rolled her eyes.

"Going after Daniel was a last-ditch, desperate attempt to get to Ronald," Mr. Masters went on. "Channing swears he only wanted to scare Ronald, that he never would have hurt Daniel." Mr. Masters's mouth grew thin. "But from what I saw when we caught Channing, I'm not so sure."

"What happens to him now?" asked Stacey.

"He's being held for psychiatric observation," said Mr. Masters. "Then we'll see."

"And Mr. Pierce?" I prompted him.

"We're going to give story credit to Mr. Channing and Mr. Pierce. Mr. Channing will be paid appropriately."

"Good thing," I heard Abby mutter. "He's going to need it for lawyers."

"Mr. Pierce will keep teaching, but his screenwriting career is over."

I nodded, satisfied.

Mr. Masters stood up. "And that's it." He smiled. "If someone had submitted this trip to me as a movie idea, I would have said it was too crazy to be believed. Shows you what I know."

We emerged from the limo and cameras flashed.

"Who're they?" I heard someone ask.

"Stars," a different voice replied.

I hid a smile. We were just baby-sitters, but we were enjoying star treatment, including a ride in the director's limo. Stacey, Abby, and I walked into the theater with Rock Harding — and Derek, Nicky, Greg, David Michael, Linny, James, and Buddy.

"Wave," said Derek. "Smile."

We looked at him. He was the expert. We waved and smiled.

I enjoyed it.

Maybe, I thought, as we settled into our places and the theater grew dark and quiet, I'll be a movie director someday. I liked the idea. There would be lots of people to boss around, and creating the special effects would be super. Mal could write. Stacey could be the financial manager. Claudia could design sets and costumes. Dawn could cater. Abby could manage the stunts. Maybe Logan could help. Jessi could be one of the stars. And I would make Shannon and Mary Anne executive producers.

The more I thought about the idea, the better I liked it. As the title of the movie, *Night Train to Charleston*, came up on the screen, I imagined all our names up there — with my name at the top as the director.

Yes, definitely. The Baby-sitters Club forever, I thought, and settled back to enjoy the movie.

Ann M. Martin

About the Author

ANN MATTHEWS MARTIN was born on August 12, 1955. She grew up in Princeton, NJ, with her parents and her younger sister, Jane.

Although Ann used to be a teacher and then an editor of children's books, she's now a full-time writer. She gets the ideas for her books from many different places. Some are based on personal experiences. Others are based on childhood memories and feelings. Many are written about contemporary problems or events.

All of Ann's characters, even the members of the Baby-sitters Club, are made up. (So is Stoneybrook.) But many of her characters are based on real people. Sometimes Ann names her characters after people she knows, other times she chooses names she likes.

In addition to the Baby-sitters Club books, Ann Martin has written many other books for children. Her favorite is *Ten Kids, No Pets* because she loves big families and she loves animals. Her favorite Baby-sitters Club book is *Kristy's Big Day*. (By the way, Kristy is her favorite baby-sitter!)

Ann M. Martin now lives in New York with her cats, Gussie and Woody. Her hobbies are reading, sewing, and needlework — especially making clothes for children.

Look for Mystery #31

MARY ANNE AND THE
MUSIC BOX SECRET

After I'd worked awhile on the shelves, I
turned to the records, carrying loads of them
up the stairs. Fifteen loads, to be exact. Records
are heavy, and *wet* records are even worse. And
Granny and Pop-Pop own a lot of records.
Their jackets were wet, but I was hoping that
the records themselves were undamaged. We'd
have to spread them out to dry and hope for
the best.

When I finally finished with the records I
went back to the shelves. I'd just finished clear-
ing one of the lower ones when I noticed something odd about the paneled wall that provided
the backing for the shelving unit. In one spot,
the paneling looked a little crooked. Just a little.
It was nothing you'd ever notice, as long as the
shelf was full. I reached back to touch it, and
a piece of the paneling fell forward, revealing a

space behind it. A little cubby hold. What could be inside? I reached in and felt around. At first I thought the space was empty. Then my hand found a corner of something, and I reached in deeper with both hands and pulled out a box.

A tightly wrapped, slightly soggy box about the size and shape of a toaster. I turned it over in my hands. Then I gasped. Written across the top in bold black letters (a little runny from the dampness) was the following warning:

DO NOT OPEN OR YOU WILL BE
CURSED

Read all the books
about **Kristy**
in the Baby-sitters Club series
by Ann M. Martin

More titles...

THE BABY-SITTERS CLUB®

by Ann M. Martin

Collect and read these exciting BSC Super Specials, Mysteries, and Super Mysteries along with your favorite Baby-sitters Club books!

BSC Super Specials

❑ BBK44240-6	Baby-sitters on Board! Super Special #1	$3.95
❑ BBK44239-2	Baby-sitters' Summer Vacation Super Special #2	$3.95
❑ BBK43973-1	Baby-sitters' Winter Vacation Super Special #3	$3.95
❑ BBK42493-9	Baby-sitters' Island Adventure Super Special #4	$3.95
❑ BBK43575-2	California Girls! Super Special #5	$3.95
❑ BBK43576-0	New York, New York! Super Special #6	$4.50
❑ BBK44963-X	Snowbound! Super Special #7	$3.95
❑ BBK44962-X	Baby-sitters at Shadow Lake Super Special #8	$3.95
❑ BBK45661-X	Starring The Baby-sitters Club! Super Special #9	$3.95
❑ BBK45674-1	Sea City, Here We Come! Super Special #10	$3.95
❑ BBK47015-9	The Baby-sitters Remember Super Special #11	$3.95
❑ BBK48308-0	Here Come the Bridesmaids! Super Special #12	$3.95
❑ BBK22883-8	Aloha, Baby-sitters! Super Special #13	$4.50

BSC Mysteries

❑ BAI44084-5	#1 Stacey and the Missing Ring	$3.50
❑ BAI44085-3	#2 Beware Dawn!	$3.50
❑ BAI44799-8	#3 Mallory and the Ghost Cat	$3.50
❑ BAI44800-5	#4 Kristy and the Missing Child	$3.50
❑ BAI44801-3	#5 Mary Anne and the Secret in the Attic	$3.50
❑ BAI44961-3	#6 The Mystery at Claudia's House	$3.50
❑ BAI44960-5	#7 Dawn and the Disappearing Dogs	$3.50
❑ BAI44959-1	#8 Jessi and the Jewel Thieves	$3.50
❑ BAI44958-3	#9 Kristy and the Haunted Mansion	$3.50
❑ BAI45696-2	#10 Stacey and the Mystery Money	$3.50
❑ BAI47049-3	#11 Claudia and the Mystery at the Museum	$3.50

More titles ➡

The Baby-sitters Club books continued...

❏ BAI47050-7	#12 Dawn and the Surfer Ghost	$3.50
❏ BAI47051-5	#13 Mary Anne and the Library Mystery	$3.50
❏ BAI47052-3	#14 Stacey and the Mystery at the Mall	$3.50
❏ BAI47053-1	#15 Kristy and the Vampires	$3.50
❏ BAI47054-X	#16 Claudia and the Clue in the Photograph	$3.99
❏ BAI48232-7	#17 Dawn and the Halloween Mystery	$3.50
❏ BAI48233-5	#18 Stacey and the Mystery at the Empty House	$3.50
❏ BAI48234-3	#19 Kristy and the Missing Fortune	$3.50
❏ BAI48309-9	#20 Mary Anne and the Zoo Mystery	$3.50
❏ BAI48310-2	#21 Claudia and the Recipe for Danger	$3.50
❏ BAI22866-8	#22 Stacey and the Haunted Masquerade	$3.50
❏ BAI22867-6	#23 Abby and the Secret Society	$3.99
❏ BAI22868-4	#24 Mary Anne and the Silent Witness	$3.99
❏ BAI22869-2	#25 Kristy and the Middle School Vandal	$3.99
❏ BAI22870-6	#26 Dawn Schafer, Undercover Baby-sitter	$3.99
❏ BAI69175-9	#27 Claudia and the Lighthouse Ghost	$3.99
❏ BAI69176-7	#28 Abby and the Mystery Baby	$3.99
❏ BAI69177-5	#29 Stacey and the Fashion Victim	$3.99
❏ BAI69178-3	#30 Kristy and the Mystery Train	$3.99

BSC Super Mysteries

❏ BAI48311-0	Baby-sitters' Haunted House Super Mystery #1	$3.99
❏ BAI22871-4	Baby-sitters Beware Super Mystery #2	$3.99
❏ BAI69180-5	Baby-sitters' Fright Night Super Mystery #3	$4.50

THE BABY-SITTERS CLUB®

Collect 'em all!

100 (and more)
Reasons to Stay Friends Forever!

More titles... ➤

The Baby-sitters Club titles continued...

❏ MG22872-2	#88	Farewell, Dawn	$3.50
❏ MG22873-0	#89	Kristy and the Dirty Diapers	$3.50
❏ MG22874-9	#90	Welcome to the BSC, Abby	$3.99
❏ MG22875-1	#91	Claudia and the First Thanksgiving	$3.50
❏ MG22876-5	#92	Mallory's Christmas Wish	$3.50
❏ MG22877-3	#93	Mary Anne and the Memory Garden	$3.99
❏ MG22878-1	#94	Stacey McGill, Super Sitter	$3.99
❏ MG22879-X	#95	Kristy + Bart = ?	$3.99
❏ MG22880-3	#96	Abby's Lucky Thirteen	$3.99
❏ MG22881-1	#97	Claudia and the World's Cutest Baby	$3.99
❏ MG22882-X	#98	Dawn and Too Many Sitters	$3.99
❏ MG69205-4	#99	Stacey's Broken Heart	$3.99
❏ MG69206-2	#100	Kristy's Worst Idea	$3.99
❏ MG69207-0	#101	Claudia Kishi, Middle School Dropout	$3.99
❏ MG69208-9	#102	Mary Anne and the Little Princess	$3.99
❏ MG69209-7	#103	Happy Holidays, Jessi	$3.99
❏ MG69210-0	#104	Abby's Twin	$3.99
❏ MG69211-9	#105	Stacey the Math Whiz	$3.99
❏ MG69212-7	#106	Claudia, Queen of the Seventh Grade	$3.99
❏ MG69213-5	#107	Mind Your Own Business, Kristy!	$3.99
❏ MG69214-3	#108	Don't Give Up, Mallory	$3.99
❏ MG69215-1	#109	Mary Anne to the Rescue	$3.99
❏ MG45575-3		Logan's Story Special Edition Readers' Request	$3.25
❏ MG47118-X		Logan Bruno, Boy Baby-sitter	
		Special Edition Readers' Request	$3.50
❏ MG47756-0		Shannon's Story Special Edition	$3.50
❏ MG47686-6		The Baby-sitters Club Guide to Baby-sitting	$3.25
❏ MG47314-X		The Baby-sitters Club Trivia and Puzzle Fun Book	$2.50
❏ MG48400-1		BSC Portrait Collection: Claudia's Book	$3.50
❏ MG22864-1		BSC Portrait Collection: Dawn's Book	$3.50
❏ MG69181-3		BSC Portrait Collection: Kristy's Book	$3.99
❏ MG22865-X		BSC Portrait Collection: Mary Anne's Book	$3.99
❏ MG48399-4		BSC Portrait Collection: Stacey's Book	$3.50
❏ MG92713-2		The Complete Guide to The Baby-sitters Club	$4.95
❏ MG47151-1		The Baby-sitters Club Chain Letter	$14.95
❏ MG48295-5		The Baby-sitters Club Secret Santa	$14.95
❏ MG45074-3		The Baby-sitters Club Notebook	$2.50
❏ MG44783-1		The Baby-sitters Club Postcard Book	$4.95

Available wherever you buy books...or use this order form.